the maintenance of headway

the maintenance of headway

MAGNUS MILLS

BLOOMSBURY

LONDON · BERLIN · NEW YORK

First published in Great Britain 2009

Copyright © 2009 by Magnus Mills

The moral right of the author has been asserted

This is a work of fiction. The names, characters, incidents and
institutions portrayed are the product of the author's imagination
and any resemblance to events, localities, institutions, or
actual persons, living or dead, is entirely coincidental

Bloomsbury Publishing Plc
36 Soho Square
London W1D 3QY

www.bloomsbury.com

Bloomsbury Publishing, London, New York and Berlin

A CIP catalogue record for this book is available from the British Library

ISBN 978 1 4088 0035 5

10 9 8 7 6 5 4 3 2 1

Typeset by Hewer Text UK Ltd, Edinburgh
Printed in Great Britain by Clays Ltd, St Ives plc

The paper this book is printed on is certified by the 1996 Forest Stewardship
Council A.C. (FSC). It is ancient-forest friendly. The printer holds
FSC chain of custody SGS-COC-2061

Mixed Sources
Product group from well-managed
forests and other controlled sources
www.fsc.org Cert no. SGS-COC-2061
© 1996 Forest Stewardship Council

For S. M. P.

1

'There's no excuse for being early,' said Breslin.

'No, I suppose not.'

'None whatsoever.'

'No.'

'It is forbidden.'

'Yes.'

He looked at his watch, studying it intently for several long moments before returning his gaze to me.

'So now we're both agreed there's no excuse for being early,' he said. 'Why are you early?'

'I just am,' I replied. 'Sorry.'

'You're sorry.'

'Yes.'

'You're sorry. I'm sorry. Everybody's sorry. Well,

sorry just isn't good enough. Sorry doesn't stop you from being early, does it?'

I said nothing. There was no point. Breslin was quite correct. There was no excuse for being early. He gave a sigh and shook his head. 'You'll just have to stay here for a minute or two.'

And so I remained there, suspended in time, with Breslin peering at his watch every now and again, while my people sat in silence behind me. Two full minutes ticked by and nobody stirred. Then at last he let me go.

'Slow down a little, will you?' was his parting remark.

As Breslin's motionless figure receded in my mirror I wondered how often he'd been through this performance during his long career. He certainly made it look convincing, especially his pointed observance of his wristwatch. For me it was a rare encounter. He'd only pulled me up once previously for being early, about a year before; but there were others, of course, who'd undergone the ritual on countless occasions. Which made Breslin very well practised in his profession. It was his job, above all else, to prevent us from being early, and he was a master of it. You never knew when or where he was liable to appear, though some of us with a bit more experience could usually read the signs. His presence was most likely on fine days when the rain didn't threaten to drive him indoors. We could also expect to see him when word had gone around that increased pressure was being exerted from higher up the chain of command. Periodically we'd let each other know if he had been spotted hovering at a particular location. This could be anywhere between the cross and the southern outpost, but he was known to favour some places more than others. Then again he might leave a trail of deliberate clues. If, for example, he was standing on the far side of the road when you went up, and he ignored you, it meant you had to be extra careful coming back down again, when undoubtedly he wouldn't. You needed to bear in mind that Breslin was always somewhere, and if it wasn't him it was one of his ilk.

What had happened just now was due to a lapse on my part. Breslin and the other officials had been keeping a low profile for almost a week, and this had lulled me into a false sense of security. Day after day at this point, at this time, I had been early. And so had my leader, and so had his leader before him, a trend that repeated itself right up the line. Then suddenly, for reasons of his own, Breslin had decided to strike. Doubtless there were far worse cases than mine. After all, I was only six minutes early. There were certain individuals who could easily have been ten minutes early during a quiet spell like this, and they wouldn't have been treated quite so leniently. Breslin knew my face, however, and he'd let me off the hook.

Nonetheless, I resumed my journey feeling somewhat disgruntled. By detaining me for two minutes, Breslin had completely disrupted my momentum. I'd been drifting across the common on a bright spring morning, speculating about my breakfast, knowing I had six minutes in hand. Six minutes to do with as I wished. Six minutes that spared me from having to rush. Six minutes that allowed me to be patient with my people; even to be nice to them. But now Breslin had interfered and two of those minutes were lost forever. Admittedly, I still had four minutes to spare, yet somehow it wasn't the same.

When I got back I discussed the matter with Edward, who could be relied upon to have an empathetic ear.

'I know the feeling well,' he said. 'You're coming

in for breakfast, counting down towards your change over. You've allowed for unforeseen events unfolding in the final mile. You've got it all planned. You're going to get rid of a minute here, a minute there, all nicely under your personal control. Then suddenly it's snatched away from you. You've lost your freedom of action.'

'Precisely.'

'I agree it can be very irksome,' said Edward. 'Unfortunately, it's an occupational hazard. You must understand that there are contradictory forces at work in this industry. If we're late the people don't like it. If we're early the officials don't like it. And if we're on time we don't like it. The truth is, our desires run counter to received opinion and we simply have to accept that as a fact.'

'But when I first started I was quite content to be on time.'

'So was I,' he said. 'For a while. But the longer you're here the greater the tendency to be early. It's perfectly natural.'

'Is it?'

'Of course. There are many others just like yourself. Those who take an interest, that is.'

'Not the worker ants then?'

'No, not them,' said Edward. 'They have little imagination. No flair for the job, so to speak. They just go back and forth, blissfully unaware of the game that's being played all around them.'

'Is that what it is then?' I asked. 'Just a game?'

'Just a game,' Edward answered. 'Just a game.'

He glanced at his watch, stood up and walked away from the table, leaving me alone to ponder his words. It occurred to me that it would have suited the Board of Transport very well if all their employees were indeed worker ants, as Edward called them. Homogenous automatons would be even better. But actually we were a mixed bunch and we all operated at different speeds. Some of us were quick; some of us were slow; some of us, like me and Edward, could be either, according to circumstances. Yet we had discovered over the years that we functioned at our best if we were allowed to be early. For my part, when I was early it felt like I was floating in the fourth dimension, which in a sense I was. Being early could make the whole day pass more smoothly. It created an agreeable state of mind.

And being late, of course, was quite unthinkable.

'Is that your bus out there?' said a voice. Davy had joined me.

'No,' I replied. 'I'm not due back until twelve minutes past.'

'Well, she's sitting out there full of people,' he said. 'Somebody had better get a move on.'

'Maybe it's Edward's. He's just gone downstairs.'

'No, he's southbound.'

'Definitely not mine,' I said. 'Not guilty.'

Davy sat down. 'Got much to do?' he asked.

'No,' I said. 'Up the cross. Back here. Finish.'

'Very nice.'

'How about you?'

'Loads left yet. Eleven-hour spread-over.'

'Well, be careful round by the common. Breslin's on the prowl.'

'I'm fully aware of that, thank you. He's just booked me.'

'You're joking.'

'I'm not.'

'What for?'

'Rule twenty-two,' said Davy. 'Breach of.'

'That's odd,' I said. 'I went through the common six minutes early and he let me off with a light grilling.'

Davy smiled. 'I was six early as well. Only trouble was, my leader happened to be ten late.'

'So you both arrived together.'

'Correct.'

'Oh, they don't like that.'

'Tell me about it.' Davy went and got some tea and ordered his breakfast.

'How could your leader be ten minutes late on a day like this?' I asked, when he came back. 'It's as quiet as anything.'

'Because my leader was Mrs Barker.'

'Not her again,' I said. 'Flipping heck, she's a nuisance.'

'Yeah.'

'Not to worry, though. Breslin might never get round to filing his report, if you're lucky.'

'Maybe not,' said Davy. 'I noticed he was writing my details in pencil, not biro.'

'There you go then.'

We drank our tea.

'By the way,' he said. 'Changing the subject slightly, do you want to swap holidays this year?'

'Why, where are you going?' I asked.

'The seaside probably,' he replied. 'What's that got to do with it?'

'Well, if I'm swapping holidays I want to know where I'm going to spend them, don't I?'

'I don't mean swap places,' he snapped. 'I mean swap dates. I've got spring; you've got autumn. Do you want to swap or not?'

'Yes, alright.'

'Thought so,' he announced, producing a docket. 'I've already filled in the relevant details.'

The docket was pre-signed by Davy, so all I had to do was add my own signature and the transaction was complete. He then pulled out a whole wad of similar dockets and began leafing through them.

'I've got one or two job swaps here as well,' he said. 'Might interest you. Let's have a look.'

Davy habitually carried a number of these exchange dockets with him. There were forty rostered duties on our route, covering almost twenty-two hours each day. Different drivers had different preferences about which hours they worked, and therefore a great deal of swapping took place. Some favoured those duties which were spread over a longer period of time, and which as a result paid higher wages. Others liked to work in the late evenings, which left them the daylight hours to pursue other pastimes. My personal predilection was for dawn starts, but these types of duty were rare and you couldn't always get them. Which was when it was best to speak to

Davy. He acted as a sort of broker between drivers, arranging two- and even three-way swaps on their behalf. Officially there was a clerk downstairs in the duty room who was supposed to handle this kind of thing, but most of us found it easier to use Davy's services. Whenever I was looking for a dawn start he invariably had a suitable one hidden up his sleeve.

'Here you are,' he said. 'Two weeks' time. Number three duty.'

'Great,' I said.

'Right. Sign here.'

At that moment the canteen door swung open and Hastings burst in looking very red-faced.

'Whose bus is that out there full of people?' he demanded.

There were about a dozen drivers sitting round the various tables. Nobody answered. Hastings stormed out again.

'Six weeks' time you've got a spread-over,' Davy continued.

'Have I?' I said.

'I'll take that and then fix it for you to do Fitzroy's job. OK?'

'Sounds fine to me.'

'So you need to sign this. And this.'

I did as he asked. 'Anything else?' I enquired.

'Not for the moment, no,' said Davy.

Again the door swung open and Hastings reappeared.

'Look,' he said. 'It must be one of you lot. I've been round the whole garage and there are no other drivers about. That bus has been waiting almost ten minutes and the people are on the verge of rebellion. It won't be long before they turn into a baying mob.'

Hastings looked desperate, so I said, 'Why don't you try that bloke over there?'

In the far corner of the canteen was a rest area equipped with a television set and a few soft, low chairs. The TV was never switched off and had been stuck on the same channel for at least four years. It was strategically mounted on a shelf directly opposite the west window, so on summer evenings, as the rays of the setting sun beat in through the glass, the television screen was completely obliterated.

Slumped on one of the low chairs was a driver, fast asleep. I happened to know he was a recent recruit, and clearly he was not yet accustomed to the regime. Hastings marched over to him and there followed an unfortunate scene in which the poor fellow was woken unceremoniously from his slumbers. Then, still in a dazed state, he was ordered downstairs to take over the stranded bus. I was glad it wasn't me.

Davy and I finished off our business with the dockets. I checked my watch. Fifteen minutes remaining. Just time for another tea.

'Look,' said Davy. 'There goes Mick.'

I glanced across the canteen. Mick Wilson had just come in and was heading towards the officials' annexe, accompanied by two inspectors. They were both in full uniform and walked one on each side of him. We gave Mick a wave, and he nodded in reply. Then he was gone.

'I wonder how long it'll be before he undergoes his conversion?' I said.

'Same as the others, I expect,' said Davy. 'Virtually instantaneous.'

'I'd have thought Mick would hold out for at least a short while,' I said. 'After all, he's an archetypal early man.'

'That doesn't seem to make any difference,' replied Davy. 'Look at the way Barrington was transformed in a matter of only a few days.'

'Oh, yes, Barrington,' I said. 'I'd forgotten all about him.'

'Exactly,' said Davy. 'He used to be very much one of us, yet he accepted the entire doctrine in a twinkling. No questions asked. Needless to say it did him no good at all. Two years, he lasted, before vanishing into obscurity.'

'Friendless and forgotten.'

'Indeed.'

'I hope that doesn't happen to Mick,' I said.

'Well, it might,' Davy answered.

2

'There's no excuse for being early,' said Breslin.

'No, I suppose not.'

'None whatsoever.'

'No.'

'It is forbidden.'

'Yes.'

This was the second time in a week Breslin had pulled me up for being early, and he would have been well within his rights to throw the book at me. He was quite correct, of course. There was no excuse for being early. Today, however, there was at least a reason. During the morning a water main had burst on the approach road south of the river, and the ensuing emergency repairs had blocked the route to the common. A diversion was put in operation which sent all our buses along the embankment. It so happened the repair work had been completed just as I came over the bridge. The diversion was therefore lifted and I continued along the normal route. Now generally on these occasions the first bus to arrive after a long interval gets clobbered with people, and there were indeed a lot of them waiting at the stops. By some fortune, though, the ones who came onto my bus were what I called a 'good sample'. This was my term for people who didn't dawdle when they came on board. They knew where they were going, they had the correct fares ready beforehand, and they didn't waste time bewailing the lack of buses. They were on their way to work, mostly, all heading for the same destination, namely the underground station at the far side of the common, and it was in none of their interests to delay the bus. Once I'd served the first few stops I was packed to the gunwales, so I put my foot down and pressed on, my priority being to get these people on their way as quickly as possible. It wasn't until I neared the edge of the common and saw Breslin standing there that I bothered to check the time. I was six minutes early. He flagged me down and I stopped.

'You're six minutes early,' he announced.

'Yes,' I replied. 'But I've got about ninety people here.'

Breslin peered inside.

'So you have,' he said, before uttering his oft-repeated mantra. 'There's no excuse for being early.'

Nevertheless, I sensed today it wasn't actually the six minutes that concerned him, but rather the fact all his buses were coming along in the wrong order. This was a state of affairs he simply could not embrace. Some buses that should have been in front of me were now trailing well behind, and he was going to have his work cut out for the rest of the morning getting them all rearranged. And because I was early he had the perfect pretext to detain me.

'You'll have to stay here for a minute or two.'

It didn't matter to Breslin that there were ninety people desperate to reach their journeys' end. It was the running order of the buses themselves that interested him. He stood in the doorway examining his watch with an air of detached authority. As always he was wearing his uniform black tunic, black trousers, black shoes and black peaked cap. The people remained silent. After a minute another bus, also fully-loaded, arrived and departed again. A further minute went slowly by, and finally Breslin let me go.

'Slow down a little, will you?' was his parting remark.

I watched him dwindle in my mirror, suddenly realising that once again he'd let me off without a booking.

Back at the garage I discussed the incident with Edward and Jeff.

'You'd think they'd be grateful, wouldn't you?' said Jeff with indignation. 'Any other business would be highly delighted if you delivered the goods six minutes ahead of schedule.'

'Unfortunately this isn't a business,' said Edward. 'It's a service.'

We all laughed. He might have added that it was people we were conveying, not goods.

'What Breslin attempted this morning was a form of alchemy,' he continued. 'If he'd left the buses to sort themselves out they'd most probably have been back in the desired sequence after a couple of hours. Instead he tried to dispel chaos at a stroke, and as usual nobody gained. The fact is it's almost impossible to run a proper bus service in this city. The forces ranged against success are just too numerous. Oh, I know there are cities on the continent where buses are a byword for efficiency, and people wonder why it can't happen here. But those places are bland and featureless. Mostly they've been bombed flat and rebuilt from scratch; the roads are spacious and the populations obedient, rational and unselfish. Buses sweep along keeping exactly to schedule, punctual at every point from start to finish. In this city it's different. The streets are higgledy-piggledy and narrow; there are countless squares and circuses, zebra crossings and pelicans. Go east from the arch and you've got twenty-three sets of traffic lights in a row. All those shops, and all those pedestrians pouring into the road. Then there are the daily incidentals: street markets, burst water mains, leaking gas pipes, diesel spillages, resurfacing works, ad hoc refuse collections, broken-down vehicles, troops on horseback, guards being changed, protest marches, royal cavalcades and presidential motorcades. Shall I go on?'

'You might as well,' I said. 'Now you've started.'

'The men who dig up the roads don't care about the people on the buses; nor do the cabbies, the dairymen, the deliverymen, the road-sweepers, the wheel-clampers, the rickshaw-pedallers, the out-of-town coach drivers, the sightseeing operators and the host of others who conspire to clog up the bus routes. Consequently, a journey that can be completed in an hour on Tuesday may take an hour and a quarter on Wednesday and an hour and a half on Thursday. This puts the Board of Transport in a very difficult position: on the one hand they're obliged to provide sufficient running time to allow for all these contingencies; but then on the days when nothing happens and the roads are clear, they end up stuck with a succession of early buses. Faced with this dilemma they've adopted a single, guiding principle from which they will not stray whatever the circumstances.'

Edward paused. I'd heard him deliver large parts of this speech before, but it was always interesting to hear his latest variation on a theme. The bit about the presidential motorcades, for instance, was a recent addition: normally he referred only to prime-ministerial motorcades.

Jeff, who was sitting opposite Edward, appeared suitably impressed. He'd only been with us a few months and it was obvious he hadn't heard Edward in full flow before.

'What is this guiding principle?' he asked.

'The maintenance of headway,' replied Edward. 'The notion that a fixed interval between buses on a regular service can be attained and adhered to.'

'But that's preposterous!' said Jeff.

'Preposterous or not,' said Edward. 'The maintenance of headway is held up as the one great truth by the Board of Transport. The officials are all indoctrinated with this central tenet. It's what they strive towards, and it's what makes men like Breslin believe they can perform miracles.'

Jeff looked thoughtful. 'That explains something that happened last week,' he said. 'What's the name of that inspector who always tells you why?'

'Greeves,' I said.

'Oh, yes, Greeves. Well, it was early evening on Thursday. I was coming back from the cross about three-quarters full when he appeared out of nowhere and flagged me down. "Right," he said. "I'm going to adjust you and I'll tell you why." Then he pointed along the ring road all flamboyantly. "Carry on as far as the underpass, but instead of turning left, get rid of your people and continue straight-ahead, out-of-service. Follow the road all the way round, and when you get to the arch start picking up again." Next came the explanation: "I've got too many buses up this end and not enough down that end. You'll be pleased to know you're part of the remedy." Then he signed my log card and sent me on my way.'

'Cutting out the middle section of the route,' said Edward. 'That's their most common ploy.'

'I know,' replied Jeff. 'But getting rid of my people was easier said than done. They didn't want to go, and when I arrived at the turn-off I practically had to prise them out of the bus. It was late-night closing. They didn't want to be dumped by the underpass; they wanted to go to the circus!'

'That wasn't part of the plan,' I remarked.

'Maybe not,' said Jeff. 'All the same, I think it was an abuse of power. Greeves made me do exactly the same thing on my next trip as well. At the end of the duty there was all this mumbo-jumbo written across my log card, inscribed in his own fair hand, which was supposed to justify the disruption he'd caused.'

'The officials don't see it as disruption,' said Edward. 'Not if the purpose is the maintenance of headway.'

'But what about the people?'

'People aren't important,' Edward declared. 'Only bus movements.'

He glanced at his watch, stood up and walked away from the table, leaving Jeff and me to ponder his words.

'At least Greeves has the courtesy to explain his motives,' I said. 'Some of the officials rearrange us like mere pawns on a chessboard.'

'Do you think they operate independently?' Jeff asked. 'Or do they take orders from above?'

'A bit of both,' I replied. 'It's all coordinated, apparently, though you wouldn't believe it half the time. I don't know if you know this, but until a few years ago they had their own special telephone link. Remember those beige sentry boxes there used to be at every timing point?'

'Yeah.'

'Well, they each had a telephone inside. The inspectors used them as a sort of office, and they could all keep in touch with one another. In fact, some of them got so deeply involved in their conversations you could drive past without them noticing. Quite handy if you were a bit earlier than you intended to be. I remember once, years ago, I was in a VPB* and suddenly realised I was going to get to the point ten minutes early. It was too late to do anything about it,

* Venerable Platform Bus

22

so I pressed on and hoped for the best. Luckily, the official was on the phone with his head stuck in the box, so I put the gears in neutral and rolled quietly past without him even knowing.'

'Blimey.'

'Couldn't do that these days, of course. They're all equipped with walkie-talkies and you never know where they're going to pop up.'

'They have a roving commission,' said Jeff.

'Very true,' I agreed. 'Especially Breslin.'

I checked my watch. Fifteen minutes remaining. Just time for another tea.

'What was it like driving a VPB?' Jeff enquired. 'I've heard they were a bit sluggish.'

'Yes, very sluggish,' I said. 'Unless you happened to get hold of one of the fast ones, but they were few and far between. Anyway, you didn't want to be going too fast. The brakes weren't as good as on modern buses.'

'Handled alright, did they?'

'Oh yes, but to tell the truth the actual bus itself wasn't particularly important. History paints a very romantic picture of the VPB, yet you have to remember the driver was completely at the mercy of the conductor.'

'Yes, I suppose so,' said Jeff. 'I never thought of that.'

'If you had a good conductor, the VPB was fine, but some of them could be very difficult. Notorious even. Basically, you could only go as fast as your conductor allowed because they had control of the bell. You really thought some of them must have gone to sleep in between stops, they were so slow ringing it. Others rang the bell while there were still people getting on and off. Then there were those who behaved like martinets, forever marching round the front of the bus, giving orders. You couldn't get away from them, perched up there in the cab. It was like being stuck in a goldfish bowl.'

'So were you glad to see the back of them?'

'I've got mixed feelings,' I said. 'My last conductor was marvellous. Jumo, his name was, and a real treat to work with. Before him there was Stanley, who fancied himself as a disciplinarian but who was a real nightmare with the bell. Then there was Maisie, very nice but rather lazy. They've all gone now, of course. It's almost a year since they were paid off.'

While we'd been talking Davy had joined us at the table. 'Is it a year already?' he asked.

'Yep,' I replied. 'A year next Friday, to be exact, since the last VPB came rolling into the shed.'

'Well, progress is on the march,' he said with triumph. 'I've just seen the future.'

'You mean the articulated bus?'

'Yes.' Davy glared at me. 'How did you know about that?'

'It's been around for weeks,' I shrugged. 'The engineers have been carrying out trials up and down the old coach road. Where did you see it?'

'Spanish Infanta.'

'There you are then. They must have extended the run to see how it negotiates the double roundabout. We'll probably start spotting it all over the place soon, while they put it through its paces.'

'It makes the VPB look very old-fashioned,' said Davy. 'I bet it holds loads more people.'

'Yes, it does,' I said. 'Trouble is, most of them have to stand.'

'Won't it put some of us out of a job?' said Jeff. 'After all, if it takes more people they'll need fewer buses.'

'It doesn't work like that,' I rejoined. 'If it's a success they'll put more on the road, not less. Edward told me there were similar concerns when one-man buses first appeared on the streets. Everyone assumed the VPB would be phased out immediately because it required a crew of two, but actually it continued running for another thirty years. The only reason they finally got rid of it was because people kept falling off the back.'

' "Safety first",' said Davy.

'Correct,' I said. 'A modern bus requires doors, not only to prevent accidents, but also to stop too many people coming on board.'

'Seems a shame to me,' remarked Jeff. 'The VPB had much more character than these new vehicles.'

'I agree with you,' said Davy. 'All the same, progress is progress, and in the final analysis the VPB had to go. Keeping it would have been like retaining an air force of legendary wooden monoplanes.'

'And you certainly needn't worry about your job,' I added. 'There's no such thing as an unemployed bus driver.'

3

'Right,' said Greeves. 'I'm going to adjust you and I'll tell you why.'

Greeves was a completely different kettle of fish to most of the other officials. Apart from his custom of giving detailed explanations to every driver he encountered, he also had a very affable manner, which made him relatively popular. He operated in the area immediately around the cross, but his prime concern seemed to be with what was going on in the furthest reaches of the route. Therefore, it came as no surprise when he proceeded to issue identical directions to those he'd given Jeff the previous week.

'I've got too many buses up this end and not enough down that end,' he said. 'You'll be pleased to know you're part of the remedy.'

As Greeves spoke I glanced down at my dashboard, where somebody had written the words I'LL TELL YOU WHY with a felt-tip pen.

This strategy of sending us on excursions was not new, but lately the officials were resorting to it much more often. It meant the bus avoided the bejewelled thoroughfare, which could take up to thirty minutes to traverse, and instead went out-of-service via the ring road. Personally I found this a bit of a disappointment, because the bejewelled thoroughfare was my favourite section of the route. There were plenty of drivers who thought the opposite, of course. They found it tedious and frustrating, especially the twenty-three sets of traffic lights which stood all in a row, and which were all out of sequence with one another. These could be a great hindrance, as could the hordes of pedestrians wandering into the road (including the foreign tourists who invariably looked the wrong way before crossing). Nonetheless, there was something about driving down the bejewelled thoroughfare that appealed to me. It was a great canyon of flagship stores stretching side by side for nearly a mile. Most of these stores were floodlit at night and many were bedecked with fluttering pennants. Around

Yuletide, masses of fairy lights augmented the already vast array of street lamps, illuminated windows and flashing beacons. Congestion was endemic. There were countless motorbikes, cycle-rickshaws and taxis. All the cab ranks faced east, while the type of people who used them generally lived in the west. Accordingly, there was a continual swirl of taxis performing U-turns. More often than not, they did this without signalling; nor did they signal when executing their other less orthodox manoeuvres. (Such were the inalienable rights of cabbies.) Early on summer mornings the household cavalry led strings of horses down the bejewelled thoroughfare as a test of their sobriety (the horses not the men), before treating them to a well-earned gallop in the park. Twice daily a water tanker sprayed the kerbs and pavements to keep the dust at bay; and well before noon obstructive geezers in vans began delivering the evening newspapers. Through the midst of this tumult moved endless columns of buses, sometimes streaming along, sometimes reduced to a crawl, and often accompanied by the plaintive drone of a lone piper standing immobile amongst the thronging crowd. The bejewelled thoroughfare could be hectic at times, but never was it dull.

Today, though, my instructions were to miss it out altogether. Greeves duly signed my log card and sent me on my way.

I'd been half full of people when he'd stopped me, and when I arrived at the underpass I had to kick them all off again. As usual they didn't want to go, but after some gentle persuasion they reluctantly complied. I must admit I felt sorry for them sometimes, constantly being shifted from pillar to post like this, but unfortunately there was nothing I could do about it. Orders were orders. After they'd gone I sped merrily along the ring road, arriving at the arch some fifteen minutes later. Then I resumed normal service, picking up people who were completely oblivious to the adjustment Greeves had made on their behalf. There weren't many of them, to tell the truth, and it wasn't long before I saw the reason why. Just in front of me, at a distance of less than a quarter of a mile, was another bus!

Despite his best intentions, Greeves had seriously miscalculated, and I was now faced with a number of choices. Officially, if one bus caught up with another the second bus was supposed to hold back and give the leading bus a chance to get clear ahead. Another option was for the follower quickly to catch up and overtake the leader, and then play a game of leapfrog in which both buses travelled in tandem working alternate stops. This required the cooperation of the other driver, of course, and was usually reserved for when both buses were late and trying to make up lost time. A third approach was for one bus simply to follow the other at close quarters, nose to tail, and make absolutely no effort to separate. Understandably, the Board of Transport took a very dim view of this last practice; and the leapfrogging was hardly less frowned upon. In the opinion of the Board, two buses running together only counted as one bus. The infringement was considered even worse when there were three or more buses in the equation. Few of us were innocent. I once participated in a convoy of nine vehicles, all bound for the same destination. Such a sight could turn the officials quite apoplectic because it ran counter to their guiding principle. The maintenance of headway was sacrosanct. Any violation threatened to undermine an entire ideology. Hence, they feared if all the buses came at once, the walls of their citadel would tumble.

For these reasons I decided not to get involved with the bus in front, and instead kept my distance. I could just make out its upper deck disappearing gradually over the horizon, and it struck me, not for the first time, that the distinctive red paintwork had been selected especially for this purpose. The subject had been under debate for years. Some experts claimed buses were painted red in order to make them look bigger than they actually were. Others said it was to prevent them from clashing with the telephone boxes. Yet again, there was a widely held opinion that the man who ordered the original batch of paint was a communist trying to make a particular point. Whatever the explanation, the fact that the bus ahead of me was a conspicuous red made it very easy to keep track of.

Carefully I followed it southward, over the bridge, stopping and picking up the few stragglers who had somehow managed to miss it. By the time I reached the common I had half a dozen people on board, most of them fairly content because they'd only had to wait about a minute before I came along. Drawing near the underground station I saw Breslin standing at the side of the road. Unusually, he didn't glance at his watch as I approached, but merely gazed in my direction. He gave me a satisfactory nod when I passed by, and I concluded Greeves must have been in touch with him. All was as it should be, apparently, so I continued my journey. When I neared the garage some fifteen minutes later, however, I was in for a surprise. There on the pavement stood Mick Wilson, and he was wearing the smart black uniform of a fully-fledged inspector of buses. The moment he saw me he looked at his watch, then instantly began flagging me down. At first I pretended not to notice him, and rolled on for another thirty yards before finally coming to a halt. When he got to me his feathers were all ruffled. Obviously he had not seen the funny side of my 'jape'.

'Alright, Mick,' I said. 'How's it going?'

'You're twelve minutes early,' he said, by way of answer. 'Why's that?'

Twelve minutes? I looked at my time card and sure enough, I was twelve minutes early.

'Ah yes,' I replied. 'I'm working under special instructions.'

Mick peered at me from beneath the brim of his black peaked cap. 'A likely story,' he said. 'Whose "special instructions" exactly?'

'Greeves's.'

At the mention of this name Mick winced a little. Then he moved away from my vehicle and began jabbering into his walkie-talkie. Meanwhile, I watched in disbelief. Could this really be our friend Mick, who until only a few weeks ago had shared our table in the canteen? Who had joked with Edward, Davy and me about running early and jumping bus stops? It seemed impossible he could have undergone such a change in outlook in so short a time. Yet here he was, marching up and down as if he'd been a member of officialdom for years. He was now deep in conversation with someone at the other end of the line. As he spoke he looked alternately at his wristwatch, his schedules book, and me. Eventually he came stalking back.

'Alright,' he said. 'Carry on as you are.'

And that was it. Without so much as a second glance he dismissed me and walked off to deal with other matters. Clearly, Mick knew nothing about the exercise Greeves had set in motion. There had been no forward notification, which suggested he was still regarded as a novice by the other officials. Nevertheless, I realised I was going to have to keep an eye open for him in future. As I pressed on towards the southern outpost I felt somewhat saddened by this turn of events. I'd always thought of Mick and myself as being like-minded, but evidently it was no longer true.

★   ★   ★

The southern outpost was a remote and desolate place. In the previous century an enormous glasshouse had stood here, high on a hill, boldly reflecting the achievements of empire. Thousands of citizens had flocked to gaze upon it, but eventually it had collapsed under its own weight. The glass all shattered and it could never be rebuilt. Nowadays the site was used as somewhere for buses to turn around. I dropped my remaining people, then pulled onto the stand and switched the engine off. In the ensuing silence I pondered the ironies of life. Normally I would arrive here for a so-called 'recovery period' of about ten minutes. This was just enough time to allow me to sprint up to the tea shop and back before I had to depart again. Actually, there was a van selling tea situated immediately next to the bus stand. I'd discovered in the past, however, that the vendor knew less about making proper tea than the trained chimpanzees they used in the television adverts. Consequently, I preferred to go to the shop up the road, even though it was further away. Today, of course, I had plenty of time on my hands: twenty-two minutes, to be precise. But because I'd come here via a short cut it was barely an hour since my last cup of tea. I had no desire to drink any more!

That was typical of this job. When you needed more time there wasn't enough; and when you didn't need it, there was ample to spare.

A second bus was parked at the front of the stand. I gave my own vehicle a cursory inspection, then wandered along to see who the other driver was. Sitting behind the wheel was Dean. His doors were open.

'Morning, Dean,' I said. 'Want a cup of tea? I'm just going to buy some.' (Actually I wasn't, but for the sake of the conversation this was a reliable opening gambit.)

'No, thanks,' he replied. (I knew he'd say no. He always did. I'd offered to buy him tea on countless occasions.)

I tried a different line of attack. 'Nice view from up here, isn't it?' (The southern outpost afforded a marvellous vista across the garden suburbs south of the city, extending on clear days to the wooded shires beyond. To see it properly, though, you had to get out of your bus.)

'Can't say I've noticed,' said Dean.

I had never known Dean to emerge from behind his steering wheel during a spell of duty. He just stayed sitting there, looking at the road through his windscreen. It was a habit he shared with many of his colleagues. These were the drivers whom Edward referred to as worker ants. The title, however, was misleading. He'd given them this name not because they worked hard, but because they made hard work out of an easy job.

'They're too tired to get out of their seats,' he once told me. 'They'd feel better if they stretched their legs, but they won't.'

The worker ants had several other identifying traits. They were often seen, for instance, with more than the average number of people travelling in their buses. Which in turn meant they had to stop more frequently to drop them all off again. This situation arose because they did not understand the Theory of Early Running. The theory comprised a few basic laws which any bus driver should have known. The first law stated that the closer a bus was to the preceding bus, the fewer the people it was likely to pick up. The second law stated that the earlier a bus was running, the more easily it could avoid being late. The third law functioned in the negative. It stated that if a bus was running late, the number of people waiting for it would increase exponentially. The Theory of Early Running was self-evident: it could be proved by mathematical induction; yet the worker ants never put it to the test. Instead they endeavoured to run exactly on schedule, and as a result carried more than their fair share of passengers. Then, at the end of the day when they finished work late, they failed to claim the overtime. The reason they gave was that they didn't want to be any trouble to the bus company. I tried to explain that the company preferred them to claim the overtime because it showed they hadn't been running early, but they wouldn't listen to me. They just continued making life difficult for themselves.

I was still trying to think of a way to coax Dean out of his vehicle when a car horn blared angrily nearby. There followed the sound of a vocal altercation, further horns were blown, and then a bus came ploughing onto the stand. It juddered to a halt and a moment later out stepped Jason.

'Fucking cunt,' he said.

'Who?' I asked.

'That car.'

'What did he do?'

'Got in my way,' said Jason. 'Cunt.'

Jason definitely wasn't a worker ant. True, he came to work, spent the day driving a bus up and down the road, and then went home again; but there the similarity ended. For a start, his buses were usually empty, or close to empty, and were often seen going past crowded bus stops at high speeds. He also had what might be called an 'offensive' approach to other road users. He would use his bus to bully smaller vehicles into submission, and he had no patience whatsoever with bicycles. He once abandoned a bus to give chase to a cyclist who'd jumped a red light and caused him to brake hard. The cyclist could count himself very lucky he wasn't caught: he only escaped because Jason was on foot. Shortly after the incident I asked Jason if he regretted his action.

'Of course I regret it,' he replied. 'I should have run the cunt over while I had the chance.'

Naturally, Jason practised the Theory of Early Running, though I doubt if he ever considered its subtleties. These were numerous and varied. In my experience it was important to apply the theory selectively according to specific circumstances. On certain journeys, at certain times of day, there was nothing to be gained from running early; indeed, on some occasions, it actually paid to be late! Moreover, a driver needed to apply the theory sparingly. Too much early running simply earned the wrath of the officials, a scenario that was best avoided.

Such concerns held no interest for Jason. By contrast, he operated under a shadowy fourth law. This stated that a bus running very early was impossible to catch, and therefore might just as well not run at all. Jason was, in short, a serial early runner. That is to say, he ran early whenever it was physically possible to do so. His complete disregard for the schedules was well known.

'Who's this?' he enquired, nodding towards the other bus.

'Dean,' I replied.

'Oh, good,' he said. 'Someone to follow up the road. Want a tea?'

'No thanks,' I said. 'I've just had one up the cross.'

'Suit yourself.' I watched Jason as he walked over to the van, and recalled the first time I met him years before. I was a new driver, learning the route as a passenger on a VPB. The bus was being driven quite ferociously and I mentioned the fact to the conductor.

'Don't you mind being thrown around like this?' I asked.

'Doesn't bother me,' came the reply. 'As long as we get to the other end as fast as possible so I can have a fag.'

I could plainly see the logic of his argument. He told me it was a long-distance route and he only survived the journey by going upstairs and breathing other people's smoke. I later worked with this conductor myself. His name was Gunter and he was very quick on the bell. Whenever we approached a compulsory bus stop and there was nobody getting on or off he would give me a double ring, which was his way of saying 'don't bother to stop'. As a consequence, we usually arrived at our destination early. We got booked by the inspectors from time to time, but this was all part of a new recruit's initiation. The driver of the VPB that first day was Jason, and clearly he matched Gunter's requirements. They were both very friendly to me, I should add, and when they went and bought tea I was included as a matter of course. Gunter had left the bus company when the VPB became obsolete, but Jason was still with us. Now he came marching back empty-handed.

'I've just told that bloke he ought to learn how to make tea properly.'

'Didn't you get any then?' I asked.

'Yes, I did,' Jason answered. 'But I poured it away in front of him to teach him a lesson.'

'Why don't you go to that place up the road?' I said. 'Tea's quite nice there.'

'Can't be arsed.'

Dean's bus started up and a few moments later he moved off.

'Right, that's my cue,' said Jason, heading for his own bus. He fired it up, then sat idling for a couple of minutes prior to departure. When he took his leave he revved his engine hard before releasing the handbrake, so that the vehicle screeched away in a dense cloud of exhaust fumes. I looked at my watch. I wasn't due to go for another quarter of an hour. The official headway was supposed to be eight minutes and I was just beginning to think Jason had left me in a bit of a lurch when yet another bus appeared. The driver was Cedric. He paused briefly to speak to me.

'The engineers have been fixing my bus,' he said. 'I've been off the circuit for the past hour.'

This probably explained why Greeves had altered my flight path: by sending me directly to the southern outpost he was trying to plug a gap. As the truth dawned, I marvelled at the sheer ingenuity of his scheme. Meanwhile, Cedric was rapidly filling in his log card.

'What was wrong with your bus?' I asked.

'The back doors kept opening and closing of their own accord.'

'Oh yes, that happened to me once,' I said. 'Drives you up the wall, doesn't it?'

'Yeah.' Cedric glanced along the bus stand. 'Jason's left already, has he?'

'Afraid so,' I said.

'Right,' he snapped. 'I'd better get after him.'

I stepped out of the way as Cedric put his foot down. Then he too was gone. Cedric had departed four minutes before his proper time, leaving me no choice but to begin making my own preparations to move. I decided to follow suit and likewise 'steal' four minutes. Even so there were still a further eight minutes to wait, which required all the patience I could muster. I had a vivid mental picture of Cedric chasing Jason, who in turn was chasing Dean into the distance, leaving behind them a great long road totally bereft of buses. And a road without buses could be a lonely place. I paced back and forth, glancing repeatedly at my watch, until the chosen time eventually arrived. Then I got in my bus, started up and set off.

'Stop!' cried an anxious voice behind me.

In my mirror I saw Baker running as fast as his legs would carry him. In fact he was making such an effort that he had to hold onto his black peaked cap to keep it on his head. I stopped and waited while he caught me up. He stood there panting, and for a few seconds I thought he was going to have a funny turn.

'What's got into you lot?' he said, when he'd finally recovered. 'All rushing off one after the other?'

Baker was one of the more reasonable inspectors, yet I knew I had to be circumspect with my reply.

'Just trying to maintain headway,' I ventured. 'Cedric went eight minutes ago.'

'But you're still four minutes early,' Baker retorted. 'There's no excuse for being early.'

I said nothing. There was no point. Baker was quite correct. There was no excuse for being early. He gave a long sigh, as if all the burdens of the world were fallen upon him.

'This isn't a bus service,' he declared. 'It's a pursuit race.'

4

Jeff and I were sitting in the canteen when Davy joined us.

'You know what never ceases to amaze me?' he asked.

'No,' I replied. 'Do tell us.'

'What never ceases to amaze me is how people can stand at a bus stop watching you come along the road, and then not put their hands out.'

'Oh, yes,' I said. 'You have mentioned it before. On three hundred and twenty previous occasions, actually.'

'Unbelievable,' said Davy. 'Some of these people depend on buses as their only means of transport, yet they persistently refuse to give the appropriate signal.'

'Which stop are we talking about?' enquired Jeff.

'You know the one just after you leave the ring road? By the national archive.'

'Yeah,' said Jeff. 'Request stop.'

'Precisely,' said Davy. 'It's a request stop and about thirty of them stood there gawping at me as I drove up. Not one person moved a muscle.'

'So you didn't stop then?'

'Course I didn't stop!' Davy exclaimed. 'Nobody requested me!'

'What if they complain?' asked Jeff.

'They won't.'

'How do you know?'

'Look,' said Davy. 'If people are too lazy to stick their hand out, they're hardly going to bother writing a letter of complaint, are they?'

'They might phone up.'

'Verbal complaints aren't accepted,' Davy rejoined. 'Besides which, there's no case to answer.'

'You took the proper course of action,' I said. 'If you'd stopped you would have set a very awkward precedent.'

'They'd start taking it for granted.'

'Indeed.'

'It's perfectly clear,' Davy announced. 'A request stop means exactly what it says.'

He stood up and demonstrated.

'To catch a bus at a request stop, people are supposed to stand adjacent to the kerb and put their arm out at right-angles,' he said. 'Like this.' He held his arm out straight.

'Not this.' He poked out one finger.

'Nor this.' He stuck out a leg.

'Nor this.' He fluttered his hand like a butterfly.

'Not even this.' He turned his back and waved his arm.

'Only this.' He faced us again and held his arm out straight.

'An arm extended in full view of the bus is the only acceptable signal,' he concluded, before finally sitting down.

During Davy's brief lecture Edward had come into the canteen.

'What about compulsory stops?' he said. 'Do you always serve them?'

'Of course,' Davy answered. 'I stop even when they don't put their hands out.'

'What if the stop is empty?'

'In that case I don't bother.'

'Well, strictly speaking you're supposed to halt and apply the handbrake.'

'But that's preposterous!' said Jeff.

'Preposterous or not,' Edward replied. 'The rule book says compulsory stops should be honoured at all times, even when empty.'

'I presume we can thank the Board of Transport for that,' I said. 'Sounds like one of their pronouncements.'

'Correct.'

'But I thought the Board consisted entirely of ex-busmen,' said Davy. 'Why do they make such unreasonable demands?'

'A very good question,' said Edward. 'They do tend to be rather high-handed with their legislation.'

'I'll say.'

'In this particular instance, however, the Board was far from unanimous. As a matter of fact, the question of compulsory stops was almost the cause of a great schism.'

'Really?' I said. 'When was this?'

'Oh, years ago,' said Edward. 'When policy was still being formulated. You're quite right, Davy, they were all ex-busmen: drivers, conductors and engineers who'd risen up through the ranks. Many of them could remember the old days when buses operated on a purely commercial basis. Buses stopped wherever there were people waiting. Obvious really. Then the decision was taken to flood the metropolis with more and more buses, and the network was expanded. Bus stops appeared all over the place and it followed that some were busier than others. A few were hardly used at all. The de facto practice was that if a stop was completely empty of people, the bus needn't come to a halt.'

'Common sense,' remarked Davy.

'At this point the engineers intervened,' continued Edward. 'They'd always found that the frequent bus stops provided a useful way of checking the brakes were in good order. If they squealed it meant they were almost worn out and needed replacing immediately. Simple as that. One or two nasty accidents had occurred in the past, when the squeals had been ignored, and the engineers didn't want any repeats. Consequently the new stopping arrangements made them very uneasy. The system was far too casual for their liking. This was before they'd developed the rolling road, don't forget.'

'The rolling road?' said Jeff. 'I thought that was a famous poem.'

'It is.'

'"The rolling country drunkard built the rolling country road."'

Edward gave Jeff a penetrating look.

'Near enough,' he said. 'It's also the name of a machine for testing the brakes on buses. Shall I go on?'

'You might as well,' I said. 'Now you've started.'

'Very soon the engineers began to insist on compulsory stopping. Naturally, the ex-drivers and conductors were opposed to this: they wanted the buses to flow as freely as possible. For a while the Board was in turmoil. Resignations were offered and rejected. The arguments went on and on for weeks until eventually they reached a compromise. They agreed compulsory stops would be placed at random along every route; the remainder would be request stops. In addition, they would be differentiated by colour: white for compulsory, red for request. It's been like that ever since.'

'But now they've installed a rolling road at every garage,' said Davy. 'They could get rid of the white stops.'

'They could,' Edward acknowledged. 'But they never will.'

Jeff glanced at his watch, stood up and walked away from the table.

'That reminds me,' I said. 'You know you mentioned the entire Board was composed of ex-busmen?'

'Yes,' Edward replied.

'Does that apply to the lower echelons as well?'

'Everybody,' said Edward. 'Garage managers, assistant garage managers, schedules managers, pay clerks, recruitment officers, driving instructors, examiners, route controllers, revenue protection officials. All of them are ex-busmen. And ex-buswomen, of course. Why do you ask?'

'It's just that there's this bloke who often comes nosing round the buses when we're parked up at the cross. Acts very familiar. I know he's staff because I've seen him going in and out the back entrance, but I just can't imagine him being involved in the daily grind like the rest of them. He lacks their sardonic demeanour. I wondered who he was, that's all. He stops and speaks to the drivers sometimes. Asks all sorts of peculiar questions.'

'Oh, I know who you mean,' said Davy. 'Posh cunt.'

'Yeah, that's him,' I said. 'He makes all these enquiries like "how are we running today?" and "do you think we can go the extra mile?" There's no polite answer to questions like that.'

'I take it you're referring to Woodhouse,' said Edward. 'Yes, well, he is the exception to the rule.'

'Who is he then?'

'Woodhouse is the last survivor of the graduate intake that took place about a decade ago. At that time the buses had a dreadful problem with their public image, so the Board's solution was to recruit a few university graduates. To try and get a new angle, as it were. Up until then they'd always used this stock character in their campaigns. A sort of "model passenger". You probably remember him: "the man on the civic omnibus".'

'That's right,' I said. 'They had him on all the posters, didn't they?'

'He was ubiquitous,' said Edward. 'The Board was awash with funds in those days and they employed an in-house cartoonist just to draw him. He appeared in no end of bus-type situations. You know the kind of thing: he had the correct fare ready before boarding; he stowed his suitcase properly in the luggage compartment; and, of course, he always held tight when the conductor rang the bell.'

'Did he show people how to put their arm out properly at request stops?' Davy asked.

'Yes.'

'Didn't work then, did he?'

'It seems not,' said Edward. 'Also he was a bit old-fashioned: he had a bowler hat and umbrella. So these graduates were taken on to see if they could do any better. They were a disaffected bunch by all accounts. Most of them had tried and failed to get into broadcasting, and they clearly regarded public transport as being below their considerable talents. Nonetheless they dutifully set about their task. First of all they got rid of the man on the civic omnibus. The cartoonist, however, was retained. It turned out some of them had known him at university.'

'Typical,' commented Davy.

'Then they had their bright idea.'

'Which was?'

'A series of slogans.'

'Don't tell me,' I said. '"It's quicker by bus."'

'Very good,' said Edward.

'But that contravenes the Trade Descriptions Act.'

'Which is why it was immediately withdrawn.'

'What was their next offering?'

'"Buses are better."'

'That's arguable,' said Davy. 'Next?'

' "Buses get you there." '

'Wait a minute!' I said. 'How much were they being paid for all this codswallop?'

'Thousands, probably,' said Edward. 'The whole process was prolonged over several months with trial print runs and so forth. Lots of meetings, of course. Their rate of productivity was negligible, but the Board of Transport just smiled benignly and let them carry on.'

'When are they going to learn that you can't run a business on slogans?'

'It's not a business,' said Edward. 'It's a service.'

'Well, whatever it is,' I said, 'they were obviously just wasting taxpayers' money.'

'Yeah,' agreed Davy.

'Actually, it's impossible to waste taxpayers' money,' said Edward.

'How do you mean?'

'The purpose of taxation is to spend other people's money,' he explained. 'Therefore, by definition, it cannot be wasted.'

For a few moments Davy and I sat in silence trying to work this out. Edward was invariably correct on such matters so we didn't bother arguing.

'What happened to these graduates?' I asked at length.

'They spent many months working towards their pièce de résistance,' said Edward. 'By now they'd decided they needed to be more ambitious, so they looked for a slogan that was all-encompassing. Eventually they found it, but then they went and overreached themselves.'

'How?'

'They presented it to the Board in Latin.'

'You're joking.'

'I'm not,' said Edward. ' "*Itineris omnibus.*" It means "journeys for everyone," apparently.'

'Omnibus?' said Davy. 'But that takes us back to where we started.'

'Quite.'

'I bet they thought they were being frightfully clever,' I remarked.

'Oh, frightfully,' said Edward. 'They even produced a special poster. All pastel colours and swirling shapes. Needless to say the Board of Transport didn't like it at all.'

'I'm not surprised.'

'The public, meanwhile, were completely baffled. It spelt the beginning of the end for the graduates.

Oh, they hung around for a short while, but one by one they started to drift away.'

'Except for Woodhouse.'

'Yes,' said Edward. 'Woodhouse is still with us. Passes his time churning out pie charts and so forth while he continues his search for that elusive slogan. I've heard he's currently seeking a rhyme for "the maintenance of headway".'

5

Somewhere on the road ahead of me was another bus. I couldn't see it, but I knew it was definitely there. In fact, I could almost sense its presence. By my estimate it was about two stops away, on the far side of the bridge, heading for the common, and approximately two minutes late. I was close behind; but not too close. I had four minutes in hand, the bus stops were deserted and the sun was shining. In other words, conditions were perfect for practising the art of running early. As I passed slowly over the bridge I took advantage of the majestic view: the long curve of the river as it disappeared into the shimmering east; the tower cranes waiting patiently amongst half-finished buildings; and the distant public clocks, all showing different times of day. How many journeys had I made over this bridge? I once calculated it was roughly a thousand trips a year. Each way, of course. I knew every inch of this road. Every traffic light and every bump. When you came to the southern approach there was a slight dip which caused the bus to bounce dramatically if it was travelling at any speed over twenty miles per hour. Quite good fun if you were chock-a-block with people during the evening rush. This morning, however, I was taking it easy. I'd been out here since five past five and now I was making my way back to the garage for breakfast. With time on my side I could be the 'artist at work' for the next quarter of an hour or so. These buses were designed for heavy loadings, and consequently when they were empty they had a certain lightness of touch, allowing them to move from one stop to the next as gracefully as a winged insect moving from flower to flower in a garden. I wasn't completely empty, but to my mind less than half a dozen people counted as empty. When anybody rang the bell I treated them to a precision landing, pulling squarely into the kerb, and letting them out through the front doors to make them feel privileged. Just after the bridge was my favourite stop on the entire route. It stood at a point where the road's camber was quite steep, so that the bus leaned towards the pavement in a friendly way, its roof gently brushing the leaves of an overhanging tree.

Oh, how I liked these early morning duties! There were five such duties on our rota and I did them whenever I had the chance. They all followed an identical pattern: you went from the garage down to the southern outpost, then up to the cross, back down to the outpost, up to the cross again, then back to the garage for breakfast. The third and fourth trips were the busiest because they took place at the height of the morning rush. After breakfast you just went from the garage to the cross and back, and that was the finish of your day's work!

There was a cadre of drivers who specialised in these dawn (and pre-dawn) starts, their only qualification being the ability to rise from their beds, fully awake, at five o'clock, or four-thirty, or even four in the morning (depending on which particular duty it was). The bus company appreciated these drivers (although it would never admit the fact) and counted on them to provide a reliable service. For this reason the officials did their best to make sure all drivers got back in good time for breakfast. Today, for example, I knew Hastings was on the common keeping an eye on us. I'd seen him standing there on my northbound journey and he'd given me a nod. I also knew he wouldn't be unduly bothered if I was four minutes early. Just so long as I kept well clear of my leader.

Actually, the whole process was self-regulating. I was scheduled to hand my bus over to the next driver with passengers on board, so I needed to arrive at the garage exactly on time. I now had a total of ten minutes in which to cover the final two miles. The ordained time for the journey was six minutes. The four spare minutes, therefore, were to be dispensed with as appropriate. Between the common and the garage there were eight bus stops, two zebra crossings and five sets of traffic lights, all of which had to be allowed for as I continued my progression towards the south. The former custom of pulling up at empty stops had long since fallen into disuse, but then again it provided a useful expedient when a bus needed to pause for the odd minute. The trick was never to delay too long at any one place. The few people on board needed to feel that the bus was moving, even if only very slowly; otherwise they would begin to protest.

As I trundled on I thought back to the halcyon days when I worked with Jumo on a VPB. Jumo's sense of timing was second to none: he was easily the best conductor at the garage. On our first trip to the cross he would make sure we arrived five minutes early, and while I took the bus round to the stand I would watch in my mirror as he leapt from the platform and headed for the cafe. By the time I'd parked he would have returned with the requisite tea and custard doughnuts, for which he always refused payment. Then on the southbound journey he would control our speed through judicious use of the bell. There was many a day when I glanced back to see him standing on the edge of the platform, the wind ruffling his hair as we crossed the bridge, his hand poised in readiness over the button. One ring of the bell meant stop and wait a minute; two rings meant carry on. Jumo was very much at peace with the world: he never complained, even on the rare occasions when our bus was full of people!

Gunter was another good conductor, although I remember there was one episode when we seriously mistimed the return journey. We arrived at the common with twelve minutes in hand. Fortunately there was no inspector present, or we'd certainly have been ticked off. Even so, we were still faced with the problem of being far too early. We had to lose twelve minutes before we handed the bus over to the next crew, and as we hesitated at the common our people started to become restless. Gunter normally ruled his bus with a rod of iron, but today even he was having difficulty keeping them in check. After a few very long pauses at deserted bus stops we eventually resorted to our emergency plan. Gunter gave me two double bells (the agreed signal) and I pulled up beside a service station. I walked round the front of the bus and raised the bonnet. Gunter came and joined me, and for half a minute we stood gazing with concern at the whirring engine. In full view of our passengers we held an animated discussion. Then Gunter went into the service station and borrowed a bucket of water, which he emptied over the engine casing. Moments later we were engulfed in clouds of steam; we each gave a satisfactory nod, I closed the bonnet and Gunter returned the bucket. Finally we got back into the bus and set off again. The whole performance had taken about six minutes. Gunter told the people we'd been overheating and naturally they believed him. We reached the garage just two minutes early, which was quite acceptable.

Nowadays, of course, drivers operated buses on their own and had to make decisions for themselves.

I looked at my watch: four minutes to go, two more bus stops. A slight pause at each one: nothing too obvious. As I neared the last set of traffic lights they turned conveniently red, allowing me to arrive at the garage exactly one minute early. Then I handed over to the next driver and went in for my breakfast. As I said: the artist at work.

Upstairs in the canteen, I joined Jeff and Davy at their table. Jeff was despondent.

'Your friend booked me this morning,' he announced.

'What friend?' I asked.

'Mick Wilson.'

'Ah, well,' I said. 'He was a friend once. I'm not so sure now though. What did he book you for?'

'Failure to maintain headway.'

'The standard felony,' remarked Davy.

'Where was this?'

'Southern outpost,' said Jeff. 'He's been stationed there all week.'

'I never noticed him,' I said. 'Mind you, I was down there quite early. Probably before he started work.'

'Yeah, probably.'

'Fancy him booking you,' said Davy. 'How could he do that when we all used to sit round this table together?'

'It's the job, isn't it?' I said. 'I suppose he had to find a scapegoat to justify his existence. Unavoidable really.'

'I'm not a scapegoat,' Jeff replied. 'He's also booked Cedric, Roberto, Carlos, Fitzroy, Kenny, Stevie, Coleen, Jakki, Imran, Ibrahim and both Moseses.'

'Blimey.'

'It'll be us next,' said Davy.

'Surely not.'

'Surely nothing,' he said. 'It's obvious the power's gone straight to Mick's head.'

'It was my first booking,' said Jeff.

'Well, I wouldn't worry about it,' I said. 'You're hardly going to get the sack for a first offence. In fact, you can be booked repeatedly and nothing happens.'

'Really?'

'Yep.'

'Why do they bother booking us then?'

'It's a matter of procedure,' I explained. 'Strictly for the record. You don't get sacked from this job unless you do what Thompson did.'

'What did he do then?'

'We never mention it.'

'Thompson?' said Davy. 'I don't remember him.'

'Yes, you do.'

'I'd remember if someone got the sack.'

'You do remember, but you've forgotten.'

'Thompson?'

'Yes,' I said. 'He was one of those blokes who stays in the job about a year and then leaves again.'

'Well, there's been hundreds of them.'

'Except he got the sack instead.'

'Thompson?' Davy repeated the name as he tried to conjure up a face. 'Who did he go round with?'

'Us sometimes,' I replied. 'Lots of people actually. You know that bloke who was always trying to fix the television?'

'No.'

'Yes, you do,' I said. 'Kept putting his feet on the chair. Fitzroy had a big row with him about it.'

'Oh, him,' said Davy. 'That's right. He left about six months ago.'

'Well, he started on the same day as Thompson.'

'That's a big help.'

'Sorry.'

'Who was his conductor?'

'Sedgefield.'

'I don't remember him either.'

'Yes, you do.'

Having failed to remind Davy who Thompson was, I went in search of a bus. This particular duty differed from most of the others because the bus for the final journey started empty from the garage, instead of arriving outside with people already on board. Ten minutes before departure time I wandered into the shed and saw it waiting there in the corner. It was completely alone: all the other buses had gone. For the large part of the day this bus was kept as a spare vehicle in case any of the other buses broke down; but at ten o'clock it was scheduled to make one trip to the cross and back. I gave the bus a brief inspection and set off two minutes early. Our working day was measured in miles but paid in hours. Consequently, the wages for these early morning duties were minimal. This was a fact we gladly accepted: after all, the day ended around noon. All we asked was to finish on time. If the duty was scheduled to end, say, at 11:58 then that was the time we wanted to finish. Not 11:59, or 12:00, or 12:01. The reason we tended to run early was because we wanted to finish on time. And, oddly enough, when we were on time it felt as if we were late. This was a mindset known only to bus drivers.

I arrived at the common and saw Hastings standing outside the underground station, where peace had returned after the chaos of the morning rush. How a place could change in so short a while! All was quiet now, yet a mere two hours ago the pavement where he stood had been seething with people. It was the same every day. From seven o'clock until nine, swarms of them emerged from the escalators in a continual surge. Woe betide a bus that happened to arrive just after a train had come in. Within seconds it would fall victim to the sort of feeding frenzy usually associated with the jungle: a grazing beast laid low by predators. Even when the bus was full the people kept trying to get on, and the besieged driver could do little to relieve the situation. Strictly speaking there existed an imaginary line in front of which passengers weren't supposed to stand. This was difficult to enforce, however, when people simply kept piling onto the vehicle. In the past I'd tried making announcements in which I'd ask them 'not to stand forward of the imaginary line', but they never took any notice. The only solution was to close the doors and hope nobody got squashed. Sometimes I shuddered when I thought of the interfering politicians who were trying to get the doors removed from buses. Politicians liked nothing more than to be photographed on the open platform of a bus, preferably in the company of a smiling conductor. They assumed the pictures would win them votes and, therefore, they opposed doors on buses. The impracticality meant nothing to them.

I was pondering all this when I suddenly noticed Hastings was flagging me down. I pulled up and glanced at my watch: I was one minute early. Hastings came to my window.

'Swing her round the arch for us, will you?' he said. 'Then can you come straight back and run her into the garage?'

Hastings belonged to the old school of manners and continued to refer to buses as 'her' and 'she'. Furthermore, he always gave instructions in the form of a question, so that it appeared as if you were doing him a good turn. Unlike Greeves, though, he wasn't one for providing explanations to drivers, so I had no idea why he'd curtailed my journey. All the same it was quite a result. It meant I would be on my way back in about an hour's time! Hastings signed my log card and I changed my destination blind before proceeding joyously towards the arch. The usual mid-morning quiet spell had now begun in earnest. I crossed over the bridge amidst a light flurry of traffic, collecting unhurried passengers here and there as gradually I made my way north. It was a very pleasant ride: even the lights were obligingly green. At one point I passed Kenny Barton bringing a bus the other way, and as he went by he gave me a very odd signal. He sort of pointed behind him with his thumb, at the same time shaking his head in mock despair. He'd gone before I was able to decipher precisely what he meant, but I didn't have to wait long to find out. Skirting the corner of the royal park, I suddenly came upon one of our buses not a hundred yards ahead of me. Even at this distance I knew who was driving. I could tell by the body language of the bus. It was Mrs Barker!

Mrs Barker had been based at our garage since time immemorial, though nobody could quite work out how she had lasted so long. Put simply, she did not seem to realise that she was part of a coordinated operation, which ran buses at specific times, calling at designated stops and charging predetermined fares. Instead she tried to provide a sort of 'social service', allowing people to get on and off where they pleased and pay according to their means. She had been known to remain at a bus stop for as long as ten minutes while she worked out a 'special rate' for someone, or waited while they went back for the dog they'd forgotten, or even cashed a cheque for them. Actually it didn't make any difference whether it was a proper bus stop or not. She halted at all sorts of places to pick passengers up and drop them off again: zebra crossings, T-junctions, traffic lights (especially green ones). All the people she helped in this way thought she was 'an absolute treasure' and undoubtedly she did have a heart of gold. I had often noticed, however, that just as many people fled her bus if they saw another one going in the same direction. This, I presumed, was due to her 'ultra-defensive' style of driving. She steered well clear of other vehicles and always yielded to them at roundabouts and intersections, even if she had the right of way. Not only was she wary of oncoming traffic, which made her doubly hesitant, but she also kept well clear of the kerb, so that queues of irate motorists built up behind her. True, she had never been involved in an accident. Even so, I suspect she would have witnessed dozens if she'd ever bothered to look in her mirror. Despite her best efforts to serve the public, Mrs Barker caused nightmares for the officials. She ran late from the very outset of her journey, with the result that they had to make compensatory adjustments to other buses.

Today was clearly no exception. As I watched her brake lights come on, go off, come on and go off again, I decided I had better overtake her. The alternative would have been to maintain strict headway and stay eight minutes behind, but then it would have taken forever to reach the arch. Mrs Barker was best left to her own devices so I passed her at the first opportunity. As I did so I took note of her running number. This told me she should have been four buses ahead of mine in the sequence. Which explained why Hastings had curtailed me. Mrs Barker was supposed to be coming back the other way by now, but instead he'd directed me to turn round at the arch and cover the southbound section. Meanwhile, she would continue her painstaking odyssey towards the cross.

All this 'adjusting' and 'curtailing' and similar tinkering by the officials came about due to the so-called 'service requirements' laid down by the Board of Transport. These dictated the minimum number of buses per hour on any particular route in each direction, thereby providing a viable 'through' service with other connecting routes. Officials were expected to juggle buses to make them conform to this master plan, while at the same time trying to ensure the maintenance of headway. Yet because they only had a finite supply of vehicles, they were obliged to curtail certain journeys in favour of others. No wonder the travelling public despaired. The idea of curtailing bus journeys in order to provide a better bus service defied logic, but, needless to say, the Board of Transport had a logic all of its own. How else could it accommodate drivers like Jason and Mrs Barker under equal terms? They were totally incompatible: Jason could complete a trip to the cross in half the time it took Mrs Barker. Such evidence alone exposed the maintenance of headway as a false idol. Indeed, back in the dark ages, when buses were first invented, there was an altogether different ruling maxim: 'the bus will always get through'. In those days, every vehicle travelled from one end of the route to the other, no matter how long it took. The only buses available were the 'old heavies': no power steering, no sprung suspension, and, originally, no windscreen. Nevertheless, they plied back and forth through hail and highwater, undeterred by adverse traffic conditions; and curtailments were unheard of.

This, of course, was the 'pure' form of public transport advocated by Edward. He argued ceaselessly that the maintenance of headway was unattainable and should therefore be abandoned. In its place he suggested an organic system where each bus operated at its own speed until a perfect service developed. Perfection, he conceded, could take forever to achieve. The existing arrangement, by contrast, had imperfection built in from the start. Essentially, the job of a bus driver was to hold the bus back (but not quite as much as Mrs Barker did).

My return journey was uneventful and I rolled into the garage with forty-five minutes to spare. A gratifying end to the working day. The shed was just as I'd left it, completely empty, so I could park the bus where I liked. It so happened, however, that Steve Jennings was emerging from the engineers' office just as I arrived. He gave me a wave and I stopped beside him.

'Do us a favour,' he said. 'Stick it straight in the wash, can you?'

'Righto,' I replied. 'Night shift miss it out, did they?'

'Yeah, lazy sods.'

'Do you want me to switch it on?'

'If you don't mind.'

'Course I don't.'

'OK, thanks.'

As Steve headed off towards the inspection bay I drove my vehicle into the bus wash. Then I went round inside and closed all the windows. Next I walked over to the control panel and pressed the green button. Instantly, the great rollers began turning, slowly advancing on rails towards the waiting bus. At the same time jets of foaming liquid squirted it from all directions.

Watching the bus disappear under the deluge, I was suddenly reminded of what Thompson did. I smiled to myself and left the machinery to finish the job.

6

There was a man standing in the road holding a large key. He was surrounded by a circle of traffic cones, in front of which was a red and white sign: ROAD CLOSED. I pulled my bus up and spoke to him through the window.

'Morning,' I said.

'Morning,' he replied.

'Busy?'

'Will be in a minute,' he said. 'I'm just about to relieve the pressure.'

His van was parked nearby. He was from a water company.

'Would it be possible to let me go past before you start?' I enquired.

'I'm afraid not,' he said. 'I've already put my cones out. Can't really bring them all in again.'

I counted the cones. There were seven in total. Meanwhile, the man raised a small iron flap in the roadway. Then he inserted his key and gave it a turn. Seconds later there were gallons of water gushing all over the road. Then it was hundreds of gallons. Quite a lot went over the man's boots, which were lace-ups. Casting me an embarrassed grin he retreated to his van. This was emblazoned with the words WE CARE ABOUT YOUR WATER. When he returned he was wearing a pair of wellingtons. The waters continued to flow.

I cursed heavily. The unscheduled halt had put paid to all my plans. A short while ago I'd been coasting towards the southern outpost with not a care in the world. I was almost there. I was running five minutes early and had ten minutes' recovery time at the end of the journey, which gave me a comfortable fifteen minutes for a cup of tea. Comfortable, that is, until the man from the water company made his appearance. Now I sat watching him as those precious minutes ticked away. He seemed in no hurry whatsoever to turn the water off again. It just kept pouring into the drains while he stood there, apparently mesmerised. Perhaps he, too, was counting the minutes. At the far side of his cones I could see a line of vehicles waiting to come by; in the mirror I saw a similar line behind me. My people, I was pleased to note, were sitting quietly in their seats. How long, I wondered, before they would start asking if I could let them off the bus. Officially this wasn't allowed: there were signs on the doors saying as much. Then again, I didn't believe in holding people captive for long periods. Generally, most of them were afraid to ask in case the driver was rude to them. Instead they just sat waiting meekly. To tell the truth, most drivers weren't rude: all the rude ones had long since been siphoned off to work on the underground, where they could disappear into dark tunnels and not upset anybody. Nonetheless, bus drivers had a reputation for being rude and only people of exceptional courage asked to be let off the vehicle between stops. Conversely, if they didn't ask, I didn't let them off. So it was that we sat in silence watching the performance of the man from the water company.

Operation 'flood the road' was at last coming to an end. Replacing his key he turned it clockwise and the flow ceased. More or less. As the waters subsided I noticed a small trickle persisted in bubbling up, despite the man's repeated struggles to stop it. Eventually he gave up, removed the key and shut the flap. One by one, in a methodical way, he carried the cones to his van and put them inside. Lastly he removed the ROAD CLOSED sign. I was now free to go.

'Sorry for any inconvenience,' he said, as I passed.

'My pleasure,' I muttered.

The delay had been about fifteen minutes altogether. The road was still wet, but as soon as we got moving the cars and vans behind us began overtaking. Without exception they all gave me a derisive hoot as they went by, as if the hold-up had been my fault. This was not unexpected: the buses always took the blame.

Heading south, I became aware of a great many people waiting at each of the northbound bus stops. This didn't concern me much as I knew there were at least two buses due to leave the outpost before me. Oddly enough, though, there was no sign of these other buses. Just a gradual build-up of people at every stop. Finally I arrived at the alighting point and emptied out. Why, I wondered, hadn't any buses departed yet? I soon got my answer. Driving through the turnaround and onto the stand I saw at once that it was eerily devoid of buses. I pulled up and took stock of the situation. Never in my experience had there been a complete absence of buses at the southern outpost. There was always at least one waiting in readiness, and usually two or three. Clearly someone had blundered. Whoever was controlling the southbound buses must have received word about the chaos being caused by the man from the water company. I guessed they'd overreacted and pulled all the other buses back. Which left me here on my own to fulfil the role of sacrificial lamb.

I glanced at my time card. According to the schedule I should be leaving immediately. The rule book, on the other hand, stated I was entitled to a minimum recovery period of five minutes. In view of the waiting crowds, however, further delays would have achieved little. Therefore I decided to take only two minutes. Then I braced myself for the onslaught and set off northward again. When I emerged from the turnaround I saw Breslin standing in the road. This was all I needed. He flagged me down and I stopped beside him.

'There are about a hundred people waiting up at the parade,' he announced.

'Yes,' I replied. 'So I noticed.'

'Not for you personally,' he added. 'It's your bus they want.'

This was most reassuring. I knew what people could be like when they'd been waiting a long time for a bus, and I wasn't looking forward to the encounter.

'Tell you what,' said Breslin, adjusting his black peaked cap. 'I'll come with you.'

Then he stepped into the vehicle and told me to proceed when I was ready. I advanced along the parade and halted before the jostling throng.

'Right,' he ordered. 'Open the doors.'

Some of these people must have been waiting almost forty minutes, yet when they came on board they never uttered a word of complaint. Not one peep. With Breslin standing in the doorway looking suitably grim-faced they scurried inside and took their seats. When we were full and standing I shut the doors and moved off. The next bus stop I missed out altogether, despite frantic arm-waving from the people waiting there. I did the same at the one after that as well. And so we continued, progressing slowly northward. Occasionally the bell rang and I stopped to discharge passengers and take on replacements. Meanwhile, Breslin's brooding presence in the doorway was enough to quell any disorder. He rode with me all the way to the garage, and during the journey I began to realise that he wasn't quite the medieval despot I'd always supposed him to be. There was no doubt I'd have suffered unrelenting grief if I'd been on my own. Passengers could be merciless in these situations, a fact Breslin had recognised and acted upon.

As we approached the garage I noticed several buses either parked on the forecourt or in the process of being turned around. These were obviously the vehicles which had been displaced following the earlier disruption. Overseeing the operation was Mick Wilson, who I thought looked rather pale. I wondered if it was him who had bungled. Clearly Breslin thought so. The moment we arrived he disembarked and marched over to where Mick was standing. A conversation then ensued during which Mick turned even paler. From my bus I observed the rare spectacle of a senior inspector taking his junior down a peg or two. Then the pair of them disappeared into the annexe for a further debriefing.

Meanwhile, I was now very late for my break: I had been due to hand the bus over almost half an hour previously. The relief driver was Jason, who was standing at the side of the road with a big grin on his face.

'You've done me a favour there,' he said. 'I'm finishing on the way back, so they've told me to spin her round at the arch. Lovely.'

Moments later he was installed in the driver's seat and revving up the engine. I watched as Jason and his terrified passengers sped into the distance, then I headed upstairs to the canteen. Seated at our usual table was Edward. I joined him and described my recent revelation concerning Breslin.

'Oh yes, he's quite human,' Edward remarked. 'He may appear rather gruff at times but you'd probably be the same if you'd made a career out of waiting for buses.'

'I suppose so,' I said. 'I'd never thought of it like that before.'

'Breslin is a true professional.'

'Luckily for me.'

'Luckily for all of us.'

The following day we were sitting at the same table when Jeff came into the canteen.

'Is there a difference between early running and running early?' he enquired.

'Not really,' I said. 'Early running is the generic form. Running early is the deed itself.'

'Oh.'

'Why do you ask?'

'I got booked again.'

'That's twice in a fortnight.'

'Yes, I know.'

'Who booked you?'

'Wilson,' said Jeff. 'Same as last time.'

'He was in trouble himself yesterday,' I said. 'I expect he went on the warpath, looking for a few victims of his own.'

'How early were you?' asked Edward.

'Seven minutes,' Jeff replied. 'There was so much pandemonium yesterday I didn't think anyone would notice.'

'But Mick did.'

'Yeah.'

Jeff looked quite forlorn, so I treated him to a mug of tea while Edward provided sympathy.

'It's not the end of the world,' he said. 'The worst thing that can happen is you might have to go and see Frank.'

'What shall I say to him?'

'You won't have to say anything,' said Edward. 'He'll do all the talking.'

Frank Lowe was the garage operating manager, although in reality he didn't do much actual managing. The entire bus system worked on a set procedure and most of the day-to-day administration was handled by his sidekicks in the duty room. Frank's role was mainly as a figurehead. He added a personal dimension to a largely impersonal regime. Like all bureaucracies, everything on the buses had to be signed for. We signed for our uniforms, our lockers, our starter keys and our payslips. When we went on holiday, we even had to sign a declaration stating we would come back again afterwards. (This was to ensure the garage had enough drivers available at the end of each holiday period.) Frank, however, added the occasional tender touch. For example, every year at Easter all the bus drivers were given a chocolate egg, paid for from Frank's petty cash allowance. Admittedly our eggs had to be signed for, but it was the generosity of spirit that counted.

For the most part Frank was regarded as a 'kindly' manager. I remember meeting him on my first day as a new recruit at the garage. He invited me into his office and gave me a short lecture about punctuality.

'Look at this duty,' he began, proffering a time card he'd picked at random from a pile on his desk. 'Signs on at 5:58 in the morning. That's a funny time to start work, isn't it?'

I assumed the question was purely rhetorical, so I nodded my head in vague agreement but said nothing.

'Most people start work on the hour, don't they?' Frank continued. 'Seven o'clock, eight o'clock, nine o'clock and so forth. Not 5:58.'

This time I shook my head.

'You sign on at 5:58 for a reason,' said Frank. 'The reason being that the bus departs at 6:13. That gives you precisely fifteen minutes to find your bus and prepare it for the conveyance of passengers.'

'Do I have to put the fuel in?' I asked, somewhat naively.

'No,' he said. 'The engineers will do that. But for reasons of safety you have to check the entire vehicle. Then you have to put water in the radiator. Then you have to set the destination blinds. Then you have to adjust the driving seat and mirrors to fit your personal requirements. The whole process takes precisely fifteen minutes.'

At this point Frank gave me a measured look and leaned back in his chair.

'Now let's imagine what would happen if you turned up late,' he said. 'Imagine you arrived not at 5:58, but at 6:04. That means your bus wouldn't depart until 6:19. And let's further imagine that one of your passengers is a train driver who is supposed to be at work at 6:44. He's also got fifteen minutes to get his train ready. It's scheduled to leave at 6:59 but because you've made him late, he doesn't get going until 7:10. Which means the train behind him gets delayed. And the train after that. See how it accumulates? See the potential for outright bedlam? Your failure to be punctual could make a million people late for work!'

Frank sat behind his desk and bristled with imaginary rage.

'Sorry,' I said.

'That's alright,' he replied. 'Don't let it happen again though.'

Another of Frank Lowe's tasks was to find appropriate punishments for early running and related misdemeanours. In the days of the VPB, of course, the solution had been simple. Drivers who persistently ran early were paired up with conductors who were known to be very tardy on the bell. Likewise, injudicious conductors were placed with slow drivers. The system worked successfully for decades, but the introduction of one-man buses meant a change in tactics was required. After some thought, Frank decreed that early running drivers would be transferred from double- to single-decker vehicles. This was the busman's equivalent of being cast into outer darkness. Single-decker routes were notorious for their tedious convolutions. They rarely went directly from A to B, but instead proceeded in no end of twists, turns, loops and figures-of-eight. Few drivers liked working on them and usually the mere threat of a transfer cured the problem of early running.

Needless to say, such punishments had their limitations. In the case of Jason, for instance, they failed entirely. After a few months working with Gunter he had been teamed up with an elderly conductor called Mr Otis in an attempt to slow him down a bit. Mr Otis was a company employee of many years' standing, but after only a few weeks he threatened to resign rather than continue being hurled around the bus by Jason. Several other conductors also tried and failed. Subsequently Jason had been put to work on single-deckers. This, too, had met with no success. On one occasion he went over a hump-backed bridge so fast that the vehicle's underside left a tell-tale scrape along the tarmac. Finally, as a last resort, Frank took Jason out of service and gave him a job shunting buses inside the garage. Such a position was considered the lowest of the low, but it still didn't have any effect. Jason's shunting was so quick and efficient that all the other shunters began to fear they'd be made redundant. Accordingly, they went on strike and the matter was only settled when Jason was moved back to double-deckers.

None of these stories offered any solace to Jeff. He sat at the table nursing his tea and contemplating his fate.

'One thing's for certain,' I said. 'You won't get the sack.'

'No,' said Jeff. 'You told me that before.'

'To get the sack you'd have to do what Thompson did.'

'Yes, you told me.'

'Thompson?' said Edward. 'I don't remember him.'

7

There had been further sightings of the articulated bus. Several times of late it had been seen among the traffic flowing slowly down the bejewelled thoroughfare. Jeff spotted it circumnavigating the arch on a Wednesday morning during the quiet spell. Observant tourists took photographs of it at the circus. Then, one lunchtime, a few of us watched from the canteen window as the vehicle made its stately way past the garage in the direction of the southern outpost. The trials were obviously nearing fruition, and as we resumed our places at the table there was much speculation about what the future held.

'Buses are an evolving species,' announced Edward. 'We've come a long way since the horse-drawn variety.'

'I suppose the next phase will be a double-deck articulated bus,' I suggested. (The model currently undergoing tests was a single-decker.)

'Surely it would be too big,' said Jeff. 'The sewers would most likely collapse under the weight.'

'Buses can never be too big,' said Edward. 'Not in this country.'

'Why?'

'Because people in this country don't like sitting next to other people. Especially strangers. When it comes to buses, the more space the better. That's why double-deckers were invented in the first place.'

'So why were single-deckers brought in?' enquired Davy. 'I've often wondered.'

Edward gave him a penetrating look before replying.

'Low bridges,' he said at length. 'During the industrial era they laid down miles of railway and built bridges everywhere. Buses had to go all round the houses to avoid them.'

'Oh, yeah,' said Davy. 'Low bridges.'

'The bane of the double-decker,' I remarked.

'Indeed,' said Edward. 'The situation was tolerated for decades, then eventually someone suggested introducing single-deckers. Can you imagine the reaction? There was a public outcry!'

'I'm not surprised.'

'The traditionalists were in uproar. Nowadays we take single-deckers for granted, but at that time they were thought to be quite rudimentary. I doubt if the Reverend Birkett would even have recognised them as proper buses.'

'No, I suppose not.'

Edward was referring to the Rev. W. E. Birkett: naturalist, progressive thinker, amateur musician and, of course, creator of the VPB.

The genesis of the VPB* was well known. It had begun life as a series of drawings in a storybook the Rev. Birkett prepared for his children one snowy Christmas, years ago. This told the tale of a resolute bus on a mission to deliver some presents which Santa had left behind. Only as an afterthought did Birkett submit his sketches to the Board of Transport. It so happened that the design committee was seeking a replacement for the 'old heavies' and Birkett's ideas fitted the bill perfectly. The gentle curves of the bus were entirely in keeping with the age of austerity in which the Board presided. The new vehicles were commissioned at once and the Rev. Birkett soon became a household name. Meanwhile, the VPB

* Venerable Platform Bus

won the accolade of 'national treasure'. It featured many notable innovations, not least the fact that the bodywork comprised a metal alloy which rendered it completely rustproof. There was much more as well. The driver in his cab had all-round vision through a myriad of windows. The gearbox was automatic with 'smooth' manual override. The flooring was 'sure-grip' rubber. There was a sturdy safety pole in the centre of the boarding platform. The saloon windows could be wound open or closed according to the individual desires of the passengers. Finally, it had a heater which worked properly. Each vehicle was painted red and stencilled with its own serial number; also the words METROPOLITAN BOARD OF TRANSPORT.

The VPB heralded the golden age of the 'characterful bus conductor'. These individuals could often be seen performing on their platforms as if they were turns at the theatre, entertaining their passengers with no end of helpful yet amusing announcements. Some, it goes without saying, were more successful than others. There was once a conductor called Borrowdale who thought it would be of general interest to describe the various attributes of the bus during the journey.

'This bus consists of a lightweight timber frame clad with a single layer of tinplate,' he proclaimed on one occasion. 'It is presently conveying its maximum payload of sixty-eight human beings.'

Such disquieting observations had a tendency to empty the vehicle rather than attract passengers. However, he was quite correct about the lightweight timber frame: if your bus was packed to the gunwales and you drove round a sharp bend you could clearly hear it creaking under the strain.

Gunter was another 'character', though he had no interest whatsoever in the needs of his people. Instead, the bus was run wholly to his own requirements. If he considered the weather too cold, for example, he went round closing all the windows, deaf to the wishes of any passengers who wanted them open. This was especially so in the upper saloon, which he preferred to be filled with cigarette smoke rather than fresh air. Likewise if someone asked for the heater to be switched on, but it didn't suit him, it remained switched off. Gunter liked to show who was in charge of the bus, whereas other conductors acted as if they had just come along for the ride.

Broadly speaking, the VPB was a very sociable bus. A common sight in the bejewelled thoroughfare was a conductor on his platform deep in conversation with the driver of the bus immediately behind. (Such conversations were best carried out when both vehicles were stationary.) Sometimes there would be a whole column of buses held up for a while at traffic lights, allowing messages to be passed from one end of the line to the other. Usually these messages related to the latest cricket or football scores, but occasionally they warned of inspectors who'd been spotted lurking in certain locations.

This host of assorted aspects made the VPB very popular indeed. It was a world-famous, double-decker bus, and by comparison the single-decker paled into insignificance.

'What about trees?' said Jeff.

'What about them?'

'"When trees hold sway, buses keep a low profile."'

'Well, of course,' Edward conceded. 'You've just quoted one of the oldest sayings in the book. Certainly, the single-decker earned its rightful place in the menagerie of buses.'

'Did it ever pose a threat to the VPB?'

'Never,' said Edward. 'That dubious honour fell to the advent of pneumatic doors.'

He glanced at his watch, stood up and walked away from the table, leaving the rest of us to ponder his words.

'I thought Edward favoured doors on buses,' said Jeff.

'Yes,' I said. 'He does.'

'So what did he mean by "dubious honour"?'

'He was a reluctant convert,' I explained. 'He still has his doubts.'

'Oh.'

'Well, I'm glad there are doors on buses,' said Davy. 'Imagine driving along the bejewelled thoroughfare without any. There'd be people piling on every time you pulled up at the traffic lights.'

'Yeah.'

'Then you've got those long bus stops which take three buses at a time. If you couldn't keep the doors shut you'd have sheer anarchy. It would be nothing less than a free-for-all.'

'Funny enough, I don't mind how many people get on my bus,' said Jeff. 'It's getting rid of them again that's the problem.'

We all agreed about that. Dropping people off was a drag, the trouble being that the rear exit doors would only operate if you stopped and applied the hand brake. By contrast, the front doors swished open at the mere touch of a foot pedal. My personal preference was for a double-decker bus with just one set of doors at the front. There were still a number of these buses at sundry outlying garages, but lately they were becoming few and far between.

'Why didn't they equip the VPB with doors?' said Jeff. 'Then they could have had the best of both worlds.'

'Don't ask me,' I said. 'That remains one of the great unanswered questions.'

8

The road was clogged with slow-moving traffic. I'd been sitting behind the same lorry for almost half an hour as we inched glacially towards the southern outpost. On the back of this lorry was a sign that said: IF YOU CAN'T SEE MY MIRRORS I CAN'T SEE YOU.

I had read these words so many times during the past thirty minutes that they'd become stuck in my head. I'd even set them to music and convinced myself I had the makings of a pop song:

> If you can't see my mirrors
> I can't see you any more
> I can't see you ... any more

If you believe in mirrors
You won't see me any more
You won't see me … any more

All I needed now was an agent.

Sitting in a bus composing songs might seem pointless, but there was nothing else to do. My people had long since departed, having finally summoned up the courage to ask me to let them out of the bus. Now I was quite alone, and had to entertain myself somehow. As a matter of fact I couldn't see his mirrors, but in truth I didn't care any more. I was right up his arse, as we used to say, and that was where I was staying for the foreseeable future. The queue of vehicles appeared to go on forever. Periodically, we'd all start moving forward and hopes would be raised. Then after a few yards we'd all stop again. About ten minutes previously the cab radio had woken from its slumbers with a 'bus-wide' announcement concerning a burst water main near the southern outpost. I remembered the antics of the man with the large key and decided he must be responsible for the present situation.

More time passed, and eventually a bus came along travelling in the opposite direction. Driving it was

Coleen. She stopped beside me and spoke through her window.

'Fucking chaos down there,' she said. 'I'm forty-five minutes late.'

'Any officials?' I asked.

'Only Baker,' she replied. 'He's running round like a headless chicken.'

After Coleen had gone I reflected on her words. There were many inspectors who flapped at the first sign of crisis, and Baker was indeed one of them. It required someone of the calibre of Breslin to sort things out properly. I wondered if he was riding to the rescue at this very moment. Probably not, I concluded. All the inspectors travelled by bus, and the southbound buses weren't going anywhere. The service on this particular route was sporadic at best. Today it was virtually non-existent.

After an age of progressing at little more than walking speed I arrived at the point where the mains had burst. It was exactly the same place I'd been held up the other day: a disaster area with water flooding all over the road and water company vans parked everywhere. I could also see the matter wasn't being helped by the temporary lights that had recently been rigged up. These were meant to alleviate the problem by regulating the flow of traffic. However, it was immediately clear to me that the timing was all wrong. The only passable section of road was narrow and very muddy. Accordingly, some motorists were advancing with extreme care and caution. Whoever was in charge of the lights had made no allowance for this, so that they turned from green to red while vehicles were still only halfway. Traffic then began coming through from the other end. As usual nobody would yield to anyone else, and the result was stalemate.

As I sat surveying this scene I noticed the man from the water company standing by his van. He happened to glance at my bus and appeared to recognise me from our previous encounter. Then he came walking over, grinning as if we were friends from way back when. I decided to go along with it.

'More problems?' I asked.

'Yes,' he replied. 'The pressure became too much, I'm afraid.'

'Be able to fix it, will you?'

'Eventually, yes,' he said. 'Could take a few days though.'

'I see you've got some temporary lights.'

'Indeed we have,' said my friend from the water company. 'I was instrumental in setting them up.'

I couldn't bring myself to say anything further, and to my relief he was called away by one of his colleagues. As I waited for the lights to change it struck me that there were a lot of people who 'knew' me from the buses. The garage currently employed about two hundred drivers, and until a year ago there had been just as many conductors. I was also on speaking terms with several drivers from other garages. Then there were all the people who had tried the buses and left to do something else. Busmen (and buswomen) were divided into three main groups. Firstly, there were the long-termers like me, Edward, Davy and possibly Jeff, who were established in the job and quite liked it (despite our moaning). Next came the ones who stayed about eighteen months before moving on. Finally there were those who completed their training and disappeared after only a few weeks because it just did not suit them. The middle category was by far the largest and consequently there were countless ex-busworkers whose faces I recognised. From time to time I'd see someone from the past and, depending how well we'd got on together, we would exchange greetings. I remember once I was obliged to slow down and manoeuvre my bus round a van that was being unloaded on the ring road. As I did so I noticed that one of the blokes involved had been a driver at our garage about two years earlier. I hooted my horn to say hello. His natural reaction was to scowl angrily. Unloading was illegal on this stretch of road and he doubtless thought my hoot referred to the fact. The moment of recognition came just as he was about to make a rude sign at me. Suddenly he was all smiles and giving me the 'thumbs-up'. Quickly he came over to the bus and we shook hands and asked one another how we were. (We were both fine.) It was only after I left him behind that it occurred to me we'd barely spoken a dozen words when he worked at the garage. I had no idea what his name was and never saw him again after that.

Then there was the sad case of the man who came wandering into the canteen one drizzly Sunday afternoon. Apparently he'd been a bus driver in former times and had dropped by to renew some old acquaintanceships. He had been employed at the garage for about eighteen months. Unfortunately, nobody seemed to recall him nor any of the names he reeled off. Somehow he latched onto me and I had to spend half an hour going through a list of conductors whom he claimed to have worked with.

They had all gone now and I didn't know where they were, yet still this man persisted in questioning me about them. He also wanted to know which routes we were operating these days, and what type of buses we had. Didn't he have anything better to do, I asked myself, than come here and talk about buses? As darkness fell he finally went back out into the drizzle. I felt quite sorry for him.

Another person who only remained at the garage for eighteen months was a driver called Thompson. He differed from the others in that he didn't leave of his own accord. He was given the sack, which was most unusual on the buses, but no one could remember him except me.

By the following morning the water mains repair work was well underway. The problem with the traffic lights had finally been attended to, and they were operating in long sequences that allowed vehicles to get clear before changing from green to red. Nonetheless, as I travelled south I noticed there were still long queues on the northbound side. Such delays were unavoidable really, this being the height of the morning rush. There was simply more traffic going towards town than coming away. I wanted to avoid running late, so as soon as I got to the southern outpost I spun the bus around and prepared to leave again.

'Stop!' cried a voice behind me as I pulled off from the stand. It was Baker. I stopped and waited as he came marching up.

'You're not due to leave for another ten minutes,' he said. 'Where do you think you're going?'

'If I don't leave now I'll be late,' I replied. 'The traffic's terrible back there.'

'I'm quite aware of the situation,' said Baker, regarding me from beneath the brim of his black peaked cap.

Clearly he had regained his composure since yesterday's crisis. He further informed me that I was not to depart until my proper scheduled time and he would hear no protests to the contrary. Which meant, needless to say, that the moment I set off again I would be late. Naturally I obeyed Baker's command and left the southern outpost with marked punctuality. When at last I reached the common I saw Breslin standing outside the underground station. I was long overdue, but as I passed by he gave me the usual satisfactory nod. Indeed, he appeared more than satisfied. He was almost smiling. I had noticed similar behaviour on many previous occasions: whenever the buses were all running late, the senior inspectors seemed quite happy.

When next I was in the canteen I discussed this odd state of affairs with Edward, Davy and Jeff.

'Yes, I thought they looked decidedly jolly this morning,' agreed Davy. 'Breslin curtailed me to the arch and he was very friendly about it.'

'The truth is they'd rather you were late than early,' said Edward.

'But that's preposterous!' said Jeff.

'Preposterous or not,' Edward replied. 'Lateness is something they know how to deal with. They can quantify it, label it and apportion the blame accordingly. In some circumstances they can write it off altogether. There's no excuse for being early but there are plenty for being late. Look at your log cards: each one is pre-printed with about ten different causes of delay.'

With a flourish he then produced a log card from his inside pocket and read out a list of examples:

' "Traffic delay; no serviceable bus; ticket machine failure; extra mileage; road traffic accident; mechanical fault; road closure; staff shortage; other operating causes (unspecified)." ' He put the card away again. 'It all proves they're quite prepared to accept lateness without question. What they don't like is wilful earliness.'

'But what about the maintenance of headway?' I asked. 'I thought that was supposed to be paramount.'

'The answer is fiendishly simple,' said Edward. 'They make sure every bus is late by exactly the same degree.'

'In other words it's a conspiracy,' remarked Jeff.

'Correct.'

'So there's no point in trying to run on time.'

'None at all. The timetables are a complete sham. You've probably seen the notices at the bus stops: "Buses depart at these minutes past each hour." It's all meaningless: a line of dots and a set of random numbers; no more than a sleight of hand to fool the people.'

'They're not fooled,' said Jeff.

'Of course they're not,' said Edward. 'Neither are they ever satisfied. If the bus happens to arrive on schedule it's good for the public record but little else. Nobody believes the timetables. Waiting for buses is therefore paradoxical; hence the refrain: "the people expect the bus to be late, yet they go to the bus stop *early* and wait." '*

---

* Original source unknown: possibly from a nursery rhyme.

9

We shared the ring road with other buses from other routes, and some of these other buses ventured into the hinterland beyond the cross. Accordingly, people quite often wished to change from one bus to another. To facilitate this a proper transfer point had been established at the cross, where passengers could switch buses in an orderly fashion. Buses pulled up side-by-side at designated ranks and waited while people changed between them, depending on their final destination. That was the intention anyway. The reality was different.

Whenever we were on the ring road and one of these other buses came into sight, the bell would ring. We were thus obliged to halt at the next bus stop, usually right behind the bus in question. A slight delay would ensue as the hand brake was applied and the rear doors opened. Then nobody would get off. After a pause the other bus would move away again, and we would follow. As we approached the next stop the same thing would happen. The bell would ring. The bus would pull up. The doors would open, and again nobody would get off. Sometimes the other bus didn't stop when we did, so that a gap opened between the two buses. As a result we would often arrive at the transfer point just after the other bus had departed.

In the days of conductors, of course, such matters could be dealt with speedily. A conductor like Gunter, for instance, would locate the offender and tell them in no uncertain terms to leave the bell alone. If they obeyed, all well and good; if they didn't, he ordered them off the bus. Nowadays we had driver-only operation and it was not so straightforward. Every time the bell rang we had to assume it was 'genuine' and pull up at the next bus stop. If nobody got off there was nothing we could do except close the doors and continue our journey. This was a regular occurrence. It even happened to Jason.

'They never own up to it,' he announced after one such incident. 'You could march round the bus threatening the lot of them with a horsewhip, but they would never confess to ringing the bell.'

I liked to think he meant this in a hypothetical way, but you couldn't always be sure with Jason. All the same, he had his own solution to the problem:

'If they keep doing it on my bus I give them some treatment with the brake and the accelerator,' he said. 'Rough them up a bit: teach them a lesson.'

'What about all the innocent people?' I asked. 'The ones who haven't touched the bell?'

'Tough, isn't it?' said Jason.

It was mid-morning. We were parked up at the cross, standing by our buses and drinking tea from paper cups. Jason was in his usual belligerent mood. 'Guess what this cunt said to me just now?'

'Which cunt?' I enquired.

'This fireman.'

'Don't know.'

'He said I was driving too fast.'

'Blimey.'

'Fucking cheek!'

'I'll say.'

'He told me I should only be going at walking speed.'

'Was he in his fire engine?'

'No,' said Jason. 'He was up a ladder.'

'Good morning, gentlemen,' said a voice beside us. We had been joined, uninvited, by Woodhouse.

'Morning,' I replied.

Jason said nothing, and stood glaring with astonishment at the man who had dared to interrupt our discourse. Woodhouse was looking very relaxed in a pale linen suit and flowery tie. He, too, was holding a drink in a paper cup: some sort of fancy coffee with a lid on.

'How's our ridership today?' he asked.

'Pardon?' I said.

'Our passenger profile,' said Woodhouse. 'Is it in a positive trend?'

'Not sure really.'

'If there's a downturn we'll need to redefine our targets.'

'Yeah.'

'Or at least revise our threshold,' he added. 'Given that seat occupancy never fully represents total capacity.'

This was all too much for Jason. 'Look, mate,' he said. 'What the fuck are you talking about?'

It dawned on me that Jason had no idea Woodhouse was part of the senior management 'team'. Or maybe he did know, and didn't care. Which was fair enough. Admittedly, Jason could be churlish at times, but Woodhouse was equally at fault for simply butting in on our conversation. The situation threatened to turn unpleasant at any moment. Woodhouse, however, was a master of diplomacy.

'I'm so sorry,' he said, thrusting his hand out. 'Jeremy Woodhouse. Customer approval consultant.'

Reluctantly, Jason took the proffered hand and shook it.

'Jason Reilly,' he murmured. 'Mass transportation operative.'

'I was referring to bus loadings,' Woodhouse explained. 'The ratio between passenger numbers and journeys completed.'

'Oh those,' replied Jason. 'You should have said.' He examined the remains of his tea with disgust before pouring them into the gutter.

'I see you've been testing a new vehicle,' I remarked. 'Should carry a lot more people.'

'The articulated bus?' said Woodhouse. 'Yes, the trials have been a great success: the engineers' report was full of praise. We're planning to introduce a pilot service along the ring road.'

'Seems like a good place to start.'

'The possibilities are huge, of course, when you consider there are three main-line railway stations standing side-by-side in all their Gothic glory. We're hoping to move a million passengers every day. Even more once we've completed work on the sea tunnel.'

'They're not all Gothic,' said Jason. 'Only the one in the middle.'

'Really?' said Woodhouse.

'The other two are purely utilitarian. It's more like Cinderella and her ugly sisters.'

'Well, I must remember to bear that in mind,' uttered Woodhouse with a furrowed brow. 'Maybe I need to alter my presentation.'

He took a notebook from his pocket and wrote something down.

'I expect these new buses are expensive,' I said.

'Astronomical,' said Woodhouse.

'Funded by the taxpayer?'

'Naturally.'

'Who's going to drive them?'

'Good question,' said Woodhouse. 'They'll certainly require drivers of advanced experience. The articulated body could be rather daunting to some, I imagine, not to mention the increased brake horsepower. The acceleration is quite phenomenal apparently.'

'Oh yes?' said Jason.

'Therefore, the driver selection process will need to be rigorous.'

'Suppose so.'

'Each garage will put forward suitable candidates based on their length of service, their safety record and so forth.'

'Is there a waiting list?' I enquired.

'Well, it's still early days yet,' said Woodhouse. 'Are you interested then?'

'Not really,' I said. 'I'm a strictly double-decker man.'

He turned to Jason. 'How about you?'

'I'll think about it,' came the reply.

'Well, gentlemen,' said Woodhouse, glancing at his wristwatch, 'I really must dash. Nothing but meetings, meetings, meetings for me, I'm afraid. Good to talk to you both. Bye.'

'Bye,' we each said, and then he was gone.

I grinned at Jason. 'That was impressive,' I said. 'I didn't know you knew about architecture.'

'I don't,' said Jason. 'Neither does that cunt.'

★ ★ ★

A small but regrettable incident had taken place during my northbound journey. The road works involving the burst water mains were still underway and they had begun to encroach on a bus stop situated nearby. Accordingly, the stop had been put out of commission and a temporary 'dolly' stop set up about a hundred yards further along the road. The out-of-use bus stop was clearly marked with a yellow hood bearing the words NOT IN USE. Nonetheless, when I approached from the south I saw a group of around a dozen people waiting there. Another group of a similar size was standing by the dolly stop.

Now, the purpose of this closure was two-fold. Firstly, it was to prevent people at the bus stop from getting splashed with mud from the nearby excavations. Secondly, it was to reduce the congestion which would inevitably be caused by a bus halting in the middle of the road works. Needless to say, the people at the out-of-use stop were oblivious to either of these reasons. It was the height of the early rush and most of them were in their usual dazed state. Paying attention to notices at this time of the morning was seemingly beyond them as they stood in a huddle waiting for the bus. One or two vaguely put their hands out as I drew near. The rest did nothing at all. Meanwhile, the people at the dolly stop were frantically waving their arms in a frenzied attempt to attract my attention. These were the 'righteous' people. They knew propriety was on their side, but they could not be certain whether justice would be done.

Slowing down to negotiate the road works I noticed that the people at the out-of-use stop were gathering into a tight knot as they prepared to board. At the last moment a couple of them raised their hands slightly like discreet bidders at an auction. Then, when I drove straight past, they gazed at the bus with incomprehension. Half a minute later I reached the dolly stop, where the righteous people were congratulating one another on their supposed moral superiority. Without exception they came onto the bus wearing great big smiles. Even so, I didn't really like leaving the oblivious people behind, so I waited a while at the dolly stop to see if any of them came running up. None did, and eventually I carried on without them.

The question of when and where a bus should stop was a thorny one. Apart from the abstract distinction between request and compulsory stops, there was also the matter of these so-called 'runners'.

Obviously, if a driver waited at a bus stop to allow people to catch up it was widely considered to be a good deed. Sometimes the people even said 'thank you'. It was also a useful ploy if the bus happened to be excessively early and the driver was looking for an excuse to pause somewhere.

Confusion arose, however, when prospective passengers attempted to 'race' a moving bus to an empty bus stop. There was nothing more irritating to a bus driver than to be cruising in a leisurely manner towards an apparently deserted stop, only for one of these 'runners' to come into view, galloping along as though their life depended on it.

Runners were divided into two sub-categories: 'logical' and 'illogical'. Logical runners ran in the same direction as the bus they were pursuing. Illogical runners were the ones who had given up waiting for the bus and begun walking towards the next stop. Then, when they suddenly heard the bus approaching, they came running back. It made no sense whatsoever to run away from their final destination, yet many people did this quite regularly.

In both cases the physical definition of a bus stop was crucial. It usually consisted of an upright pole with a sign attached bearing the words BUS STOP. This could be augmented by a large rectangle painted on the surface of the road. In some cases there would be a bus shelter: either a rustic version with a thatched roof, or a draughty urban one. In the absence of bus shelters, people were also known to gather under a nearby tree or beneath the awning of a shop. Because of all these various aspects, the precise location of any bus stop was open to interpretation. In general terms, however, it was the upright pole that seemed to count for most. 'Runners' always assumed that if they got to the pole first, and touched it, then the bus would be obliged to stop. (This was known in bus parlance as 'the race for the pole'.)

Unfortunately it was not quite so simple: in reality there were many complex issues at stake. Firstly, the driver would have to judge whether he or she could stop the bus smoothly without having to slam the brakes on. Sudden halts could be jarring to both driver and passengers alike, and tended to disrupt the overall 'flow' of the bus. Consideration also had to be given to the opinions of the people already on board. While some of them might be sympathetic towards the runner, others certainly may not, and hence a balance needed to be struck. Another important influencing factor was the question of time: if the bus was late then stopping for runners would only help to make it even later. Clearly in these circumstances the act of leaving people behind was an unavoidable necessity. Furthermore, the driver may be aware of another bus travelling close astern which would be in a much better position to stop and pick them up. Whether it actually did or not was an entirely different matter. Finally, some drivers were disinclined to stop because they just didn't think it was worth it. Experience told them that most runners only wished to travel a short distance before getting off again. Besides which, the gesture was seldom appreciated: people only remembered the buses that went without them, never the ones that waited.

In the era of the VPB, of course, there was plenty of scope for compromise. Drivers could slow down and allow the more athletic runners to leap aboard without bringing the bus to a complete halt. In the past, conductors could often be seen standing on their platforms offering verbal encouragement to such valiant individuals as they ran along behind. 'Having a go' was considered highly dangerous and officially frowned upon. Without doubt it contributed to the demise of the open platform. Nevertheless, it was a common practice for years and led to the expression 'catching a bus'.

This itself was a misnomer: people only caught buses if the driver allowed it to happen.

Jason, it goes without saying, had very strong views on the subject. Indeed, any mention of 'catching a bus' tended particularly to rankle him.

'The way people talk you'd think they were big game hunters stalking tigers through the jungle,' he said. 'Or out in the ocean reeling in swordfish and marlon: "Ooh, I had a struggle catching the bus this morning!" For fuck's sake, it's pathetic! There's a fucking bus every eight minutes! What's so challenging about that?!'

'Maybe it seems different from where they are,' I suggested.

'Huh,' said Jason.

Personally I tried to maintain a fair and measured outlook, but at times it could be difficult. After all, it was much easier to keep going than to stop and wait for runners. Sometimes a kindly act could even backfire. Once I waited a whole minute at a bus stop for a man who was running desperately through the early morning gloom. Only when he ran straight past me and continued up the road did I realise he was a jogger. In the final analysis the question of runners was a matter for discretion. As a point of reference, the rule book stated that we were supposed to wait for all 'intending passengers'.

Jason's verdict was different. 'People wait for buses,' he said. 'Buses don't wait for people.'

10

We also drove at night. Our garage operated a 'round-the-clock' service (almost): the last bus didn't finish until a quarter to two in the morning, and periodically I was required to take the wheel. These late-night duties were long-haul affairs stretching over many hours: a far cry from the short-duration 'early turns' which were a doddle by comparison. Occasionally I managed to swap my duty with someone else, but at other times I simply had to buckle down and do it myself.

This particular duty started at the beginning of the 'rush hour': an hour which quite often extended well into the evening. Buses forged back and forth in pursuit of other buses. Every road was busy, and the busiest of all was the bejewelled thoroughfare, which acted as a confluence for many assorted bus routes. Eastbound buses flogged towards the cross carrying their burden of crazed people, all desperately attempting to make connections with express trains. Other buses headed for 'theatreland', or trekked out towards the estuary. Meanwhile, westbound buses charged headlong into the sunset. When they reached the arch some turned north, some south, and yet others continued west. Our destination was the southern outpost. It was barely seven miles away, but the journey took ages to complete. I often wondered how the passengers could tolerate making the same trip every day, week in, week out, squashed into buses with the sunlight streaming mercilessly through the windows. It was all right for me: I was being paid for my efforts. These people, by contrast, did it voluntarily. Furthermore, I could see the view from the bridge when we crossed it; half of them couldn't.

The style of driving required during the evening rush was simply to 'go with the flow'. This was no place for slowcoaches. Everybody was on the move, and everyone, it seemed, was in a hurry. At the peak hour a number of official 'extra buses' were added to the ferment, apparently just for the sake of it. Which meant even more vehicles competing for limited road space. In such conditions bus drivers were obliged to employ harsh methods in order to make any progress at all. Often we brought into play a special technique called 'push of pike'. This was when several buses shunted through a junction together in a solid block, regardless of anyone else's right of way. It was based on a seventeenth-century infantry tactic, and was invaluable for saving precious minutes during the journey. The passing of time was an obsession for most bus drivers. It arose from our aversion to being late, which we would do anything to avoid.

Taxi drivers, on the other hand, had completely different preoccupations. Normally their behaviour was as rational as any other motorist, but during the rush hour they appeared to enter a trance-like state in which they were unable to distinguish between red and green traffic lights. Consequently, you could never be sure if they were going to stop or go. This could be a problem if you were travelling behind them in a bus. Nobody knew the reason why they went into these trances, but recently Davy had offered a possible explanation:

'It's because they're always thinking about money,' he said. 'It acts as a kind of drug for them and once they've got it on their mind they can't concentrate on anything else.'

'But what about cyclists?' Jeff countered. 'They ignore traffic lights too, and they're certainly not motivated by money.'

'There's a crucial difference,' Davy replied. 'Cyclists only ignore red lights. Cabbies in a trance ignore red and green ones.'

'They never give proper hand signals either,' I added. 'They just pull out right in front of you.'

'Probably counting money,' said Davy. 'I've heard they've got a singular penchant for gold sovereigns.'

Davy was always criticising taxi drivers. Nevertheless, I suspected he was secretly learning the 'knowledge' on his days off. He would most likely change his tune when he became one of them.

I thought about all this as I worked my way southward, over the bridge, and up the rise towards the common. There were bus stops arrayed along the entire length of the road, and without exception the bell rang for each of them. I'd got rid of almost all my people by the time I reached the underground station, at which point another load came on board. Finally I arrived at the southern outpost to discover the tea shop was closed for the evening. There was nothing else to do except go back into town and pick up yet more people.

Sometimes during the rush there would be hold-ups at places where traffic was particularly congested. On these occasions inspectors would suddenly pop up and curtail certain journeys, much to the disdain of the passengers. The travelling public seemed to think the purpose of curtailment was to give the driver a rest at their expense; the real reason, in fact, was to turn the bus round and send it back in the opposite direction.

So it was the following day that Greeves intercepted me at the cross. I was just about to depart when he appeared at the side of the road and flagged me down.

'Right,' he said. 'I'm going to adjust you and I'll tell you why.'

Then came the usual explanation about how there were too many buses down the outpost and not enough up the cross.

'Turn round at the common will you?' said Greeves. 'I need you back here as quick as possible.'

He wrote down the details on my log card and sent me on my way.

Now, as everyone knows, you can lead a horse to water but you can't make him drink. Another thing you can't make him do is read what it says on the front of a bus. I altered my destination blind so that it clearly indicated I was only going as far as the common. All the same, I knew that only a few of my passengers would bother to read what it said. The rest would take no notice at all; instead they would be sinking back into oblivion after a hard day's work. I firmly believed that if a bus was destined for HELL AND DAMNATION the people would still blithely climb aboard. Equally, they would moan and groan if they were kicked off before they expected to be. Which was indeed their fate this evening. As predicted, they bleated like abandoned sheep when I deposited them at the common. Yet it was hardly my fault.

'It couldn't be helped,' affirmed Edward when I met him later at the garage. 'You were only obeying orders.'

'Why don't they ever read what it says on the front?' I demanded.

'You must forgive them their frailty,' he said.

At this time of the evening the garage was very quiet. Edward had finished work for the day and only came up the canteen to keep me company. The place was practically deserted; just one or two drivers on late turns sitting around waiting to complete their 'second halves'. It was entirely different from the early morning period when the 'run-out' was in full swing. Then the shed was packed with buses getting ready to leave; engines were running; drivers were marching round with watering cans; inspectors were examining their schedules books and making sure headway was being maintained. Any outsider who happened to wander in would probably assume the garage was a hive of efficiency. In truth, of course, it wasn't. The officials were more likely than not to drop a spanner in the works, despite their best intentions. Greeves happened to have got it right during this evening's rush, but I was convinced it was only a matter of luck.

'I wonder if he says that to his wife at bedtime,' remarked Edward.

'Says what?' I asked.

' "I'm going to adjust you and I'll tell you why." '

After my break I resumed work again. This involved taking over a bus on the road from another driver. I waited in the darkness opposite the garage. It was now almost half past nine and the traffic was at last beginning to settle down. At precisely nine thirty-two I heard the tortured engine of an approaching bus, and a moment later Clarence came roaring up. We nodded at each other, and he slipped out of the driving seat.

'Bus is OK,' he said.

Clarence originated from a far away tropical island. He was a deeply wounded man. Hidden somewhere on his person was a bullet hole which he'd incurred years before during pre-independence rioting.

'Nothing to do with me,' he always insisted. 'I was in the public library when the riots kicked off.'

This bullet hole lent Clarence a certain element of coolness unmatched by other bus drivers. No one messed with Clarence. He was one of the few drivers who actually preferred to do late-night duties; in fact, I had never seen him during the day.

'I like to start work just when it's turning duskish,' he once told me. 'I get out of bed when I want.'

Clarence owned about seventeen hats, caps and berets (plus a bandanna), all of which suited him perfectly. He wore a different one every evening, according to his mood. Likewise his collection of shirts, which were varied and many; the official uniform was an optional extra. Rumour had it that sometimes, after midnight, Clarence took his bus along roads other than those specified by the Board of

Transport, just for a change. This was the bus drivers' form of 'jamming'. Clarence was undoubtedly his own man.

'I'll see you later,' he said, ambling into the moonlight.

When I was ensconced behind the wheel I reflected on the very different 'tone' of bus driving at this late hour. There was no longer any rushing about: instead, buses roamed placidly through the night. Fridays and Saturdays were exceptions, of course, when the bejewelled thoroughfare and its environs were thronged with revellers who didn't go home until the early morning. For the rest of the week, though, a certain calm lay over the proceedings. Desultory buses appeared as travelling beacons of light in the surrounding blackness. On some journeys there were only a dozen passengers; on others there were none at all. To some observers the sight of empty buses patrolling deserted roads may have seemed to be a pointless waste of resources; but to others this was an essential element of public transport. In Edward's words, 'The bus should always be there whether the people need it or not.'

Buses, he suggested, were similar to the post horses of olden days: constantly ready and waiting on the assumption they may eventually be required. (Indeed, the bus went a step further than the post horse because it made the journey even when nobody was travelling.)

Gradually the evening went by. I drove up to the cross, back to the southern outpost, and then up to the cross again. As the hours passed, buses began to drop out of circulation, one by one, and return to the garage, until finally there were only six vehicles going round and round. Six buses to serve the entire route! The headway was now lengthened to fifteen minutes between each bus. Clarence had completed his break and was back on the road again. There was another late-night specialist called Fabian who was also out there somewhere. The remaining drivers were me, Cedric, Dean, and a new recruit whose name I didn't know.

One other difference about these evening duties was the fact that after eight o'clock we were supervised not by roadside officials but by means of radio transmissions. Occasionally a laconic voice would call up and enquire about a bus's position or state of progress. This was usually at weekends when city centre traffic jams could occur even at midnight;

in these cases the controller would issue appropriate instructions to any bus that may have been held up. Most of the time, however, the radio stayed quiet. Buses ran unhindered through the empty streets keeping roughly to schedule, and drivers didn't need to worry about inspectors lurking in the shadows.

With these thoughts in mind I completed my final journey to the southern outpost, arriving five minutes early. There, to my surprise, I saw Mick Wilson standing by the side of the road.

'Evening, Mick,' I said, through the window. 'Didn't expect to see you here.'

'Evening, driver,' he replied.

'I do have a name you know.'

Mick ignored my comment and stood examining his schedules book by the light of an electric torch.

'You're five minutes early,' he said at length. 'Why's that?'

I had no hiding place. The evidence was plainly visible: namely, me and my bus, five minutes earlier than we should have been.

'There's no excuse for being early,' I said in a resigned way. 'I suppose you're going to book me.'

Mick gazed at me for a long time before he spoke again.

'As a matter of fact I'm not going to book you,' he said. 'Instead I'm going to offer a word of advice.'

'Oh yes?'

'Tell me something,' he continued. 'Do you believe in the maintenance of headway?'

'Of course,' I said.

'Truly believe?'

'Yes,' I answered. 'Why do you ask?'

'Because you've recently been associating with a known dissident.'

'You mean Edward?'

'I'm not saying who,' Mick rejoined. 'Merely that you seem to have been led astray by this individual.'

'But he's my friend.'

'Friend or no friend,' said Mick. 'You should keep well away from him. Not only for your own sake, but for the sake of the entire bus service.'

'This is ridiculous,' I protested. 'Edward is a busman through and through. He's only seeking improvement by alternative methods.'

At these words Mick appeared to undergo some sort of electric shock. His face went completely blank and the pupils of his eyes dilated. Furthermore, he ceased breathing for several seconds. When at last he spoke again his voice was cold and flat. 'There are no alternative methods,' he said. 'The only true path is the maintenance of headway.'

A long silence followed, during which the bleak winds of night played around the idling bus. Sensing I may have pushed the argument too far I decided to attempt a compromise.

'Alright,' I offered. 'I'll try not to be early tomorrow night.'

Mick, meanwhile, was quickly recovering his composure.

'Give me your log card, will you?' he said.

I handed it over and he wrote something in the 'remarks' box. Then he passed it back and vanished into the darkness.

I peered at the card. Mick had written only one word: ADVISED.

By the next evening the weather had begun to deteriorate. Yesterday's sunshine was rapidly forgotten as heavy rain moved in from the west. The prospects for rush-hour travellers was formally classified as 'grim'. Not only did they have to endure the usual torments of jostling crowds and packed buses: now they had to contend with repeated downpours and the resulting puddles everywhere. As the drains reached capacity I watched the people's struggles from my warm, dry vantage point. In these conditions the job of a bus driver suddenly came into its own. Waiting passengers were genuinely pleased to see us when we arrived. They regarded the bus as a safe haven from the rain and clambered thankfully aboard. Reality returned when they got off again (especially if they'd left their umbrella behind).

By late evening, however, the constant rain was beginning to cause problems for some drivers too. About half past eleven I was working my way towards the southern outpost when the cab radio crackled into life.

'We've had a bus gone missing from our radar screen,' announced the controller. 'I'm looking for running number three: can I have a response please?'

(They didn't really have a radar, of course: this was simply a figure of speech.)

After a short delay another voice could be heard.

'Running number three receiving,' it said. 'Over.'

I didn't recognise the voice, and therefore guessed it must belong to the new driver. It was most unusual to be able to hear both sides of a conversation and I presumed the radio was stuck on an open channel. (I wasn't sure whether this was due to the weather.)

'What's your location, number three?'

'About a mile from the southern outpost,' came the reply. 'Heading north.'

'What's happened?'

'My windscreen wipers have packed in. I can't see to drive so I've had to stop.'

'What have you done with your people?' enquired the controller.

'They're still here with me,' said the new driver. 'I keep telling them there'll be another bus along in a minute, but it's almost half an hour now and there's no sign of one.'

The poor bloke sounded quite desperate. It was an unenviable predicament for a driver to be marooned with a load of passengers. Why, I wondered, hadn't the next bus arrived to take them off his hands? I got my answer a few minutes later when I came upon Cedric, parked at the side of the road with his hazard lights flashing. I pulled alongside him and asked what the trouble was.

'The back doors keep opening and closing of their own accord,' he answered. 'This bus isn't going anywhere.'

Behind him I could just discern the doors swishing open, then closed, then open again.

'There's another driver stranded up the road as well,' I remarked.

'Yeah,' said Cedric. 'I heard it on the radio.'

I bade him farewell and continued on my way. This was beginning to look very bad. A little further along I passed the stricken northbound bus. Inside was a group of about thirty passengers, along with a very sorry-looking driver. The rain now seemed even heavier than before.

What I couldn't quite work out was how this new recruit came to have so many people on board in the first place. Normally on a wet night like this there would hardly be anybody bothering to travel. Even allowing for the long gap between buses it was an uncommonly large number. The only conclusion I could draw was that the new driver had been running late even before his windscreen wipers stopped working. He had plainly fallen victim to the Law of Cumulative Lateness: late buses always carried more passengers; therefore, once a bus was late it could only become later still. Now, it seemed, his lateness was compounded beyond redemption.

What was also becoming clear was that the next bus in the sequence was mine. The three other functioning buses were somewhere at the northern end of the route, their drivers probably unaware of the critical situation in the south. The stranded driver had assured his people that another bus was coming to save them from their plight, and in a sense he was correct. Yet prophesying buses was a perilous exercise. I still had to complete my southbound journey before I turned around and headed the other way again. The bus he had foretold would be a long time coming.

Eventually I arrived at the southern outpost and paused briefly. There were no 'intending passengers' at the bus stop; neither were any officials to be seen. The absence of Mick Wilson and his comrades on such a horrid night was quite noticeable: inspectors of buses, I'm afraid to say, were merely fairweather friends.

A few moments later I set off north. By my estimate the people in the faulty bus had been waiting for almost forty-five minutes when at last I approached. I could see their anxious faces peering through the rear window as I drew up. Most anxious of all, of course, was their driver. Frantically, he leapt from his bus and began flagging me down, thinking perhaps that I wasn't going to stop.

I halted and he ran over to my window.

'Thank goodness you've come,' he said. 'It feels like I've been with this lot forever.'

'Well, it's all over now,' I replied. 'Do you want to transfer them?'

'Yeah, please.'

Quickly he returned to the other vehicle. Then, in the pouring rain, I watched as he led his people to the promised bus.

11

'There's no excuse for being early,' said Breslin.

'No, I suppose not.'

'None whatsoever.'

'No.'

'It is forbidden.'

'Yes.'

Breslin had surprised Jeff, Davy and me by unexpectedly joining us at our table. It was rare for him to make an appearance in the canteen, let alone sit down with the drivers, yet here he was: he'd even forked out and bought us a mug of tea apiece.

Now he sat silently beside us, holding his black peaked cap in his hands and turning it gradually round and round. The conversation during the past few minutes, needless to say, had been quite stilted. Initially it wasn't too difficult: Breslin had begun by telling us of the latest developments with the articulated bus. Apparently, the new vehicle had been fully approved by the Board of Transport and was now ready to enter regular service. His personal opinion of the bus was ambiguous. Yes, he said, it would carry a lot more people; but, no, he certainly didn't like the look of it. There then followed some general observations about how drivers were always suspicious of new buses: he recalled that even the VPB had been greeted reluctantly at first. After this, however, Breslin's manner seemed to become more sombre. Something was clearly playing on his mind, and suddenly, for no obvious reason, he began reciting his standard litany. There was, he repeated, no excuse for being early. Oddly enough, I wasn't sure whether he was trying to convince us, or himself.

He continued rotating his cap until he came to his gilded badge of office, which he examined closely for a long while, as if it held some significant meaning.

At this juncture, Jeff attempted to lighten the mood. 'What if a bus was already early when you took it over?' he suggested. 'That would be a valid excuse.'

Breslin gave no sign of having heard what Jeff said. He just continued studying his badge.

Davy, I noticed, had begun to turn quite pale. He evidently regarded Breslin's presence as a sort of trial by ordeal. For my part, I was beginning to wonder what all this was leading up to.

Eventually, Breslin broke the silence.

'I take it you're all familiar with the maintenance of headway?' he said.

'Yes,' we each replied.

'And you understand there is a subtext?' he continued. 'Namely, the separation of buses.'

We all nodded.

'Well, obviously we have to separate buses,' Breslin declared. 'Stands to reason: otherwise they'd all turn up in clumps.' He gave a long sigh. 'The trouble is, some of these young inspectors don't realise there needs to be a certain amount of slack in the system. They've started taking matters to extremes. They don't seem to grasp that strictly applying the letter of the law is …'

Breslin faltered. He appeared to be lost for words.

'Impracticable?' I offered.

'Impossible,' said Breslin. He shook his head slowly, and sighed again. 'The maintenance of headway is not an iron rule,' he announced.

'What is it then?' Jeff enquired.

'It's merely a guiding principle,' said Breslin. 'The function of inspectors is to act as lubricants in the mechanism. We were never meant to be oppressors; we're supposed to assist drivers in carrying out their duties. When exigencies arise we make appropriate adjustments. For most of the time, though, it's a simple case of give and take. Words such as "cooperation" and "tolerance" come to mind. Yet recently certain upstarts have emerged from our ranks whose aim apparently is to interfere wherever possible. They're threatening to spoil everything. They wish to turn the arch, the circus and the cross into their own personal fiefdoms. And the maintenance of headway is their creed.'

He glanced at his watch, stood up and walked away from the table, leaving the three of us to ponder his words.

'Blimey,' murmured Davy. 'I never thought I'd hear him talk like that.'

'Nor me,' I said.

'Do you think he was referring to Mick Wilson?' asked Jeff.

'Probably.'

'And others of the same stamp,' said Davy.

'Here comes Edward,' said Jeff.

In the few moments since Breslin's departure, Edward had entered the canteen. He purchased four mugs of tea before taking his place at the table.

'What was Breslin doing up here?' he enquired. 'I've just passed him on the stairs.'

'Not sure really,' I answered. 'He seemed to be having an introspective moment.'

'Oh yes?'

'Casting doubts on his own authority.'

'Really?'

Edward stirred his tea thoughtfully.

'He was questioning the maintenance of headway,' said Davy.

'Well, well, well,' said Edward. 'Heresy.'

'I thought he was just calling for moderation,' said Jeff. 'After all, buses have to be separated to some extent.'

'They can't be separated,' Edward replied. 'The authorities have been trying to separate buses for half a century, and the result has always been abject failure. It's a known fact. When buses come, they come not single spies but in battalions.'

'Gravitational attraction,' I remarked. 'Buses are drawn naturally into clusters.'

'Correct,' said Edward. 'The most common grouping arises from the so-called Three Bears syndrome: one bus running early, one running late, and one running exactly on time. In consequence, three run together. There are, however, many other combinations.'

'Talking about running early,' said Davy. 'Has anybody seen Jason recently?'

'No,' I said. 'I haven't.'

'Nor me,' said Jeff. 'Why?'

'I had a nice little duty swap lined up for him,' said Davy, 'but his name seems to have disappeared off the rota.'

'What?' I said. 'Disappeared completely?'

'Yep.'

This piece of news triggered a debate about what might have become of Jason; and Breslin's recent visitation was swiftly forgotten.

'Jason was quite interested in the articulated bus,' I said. 'Perhaps he's applied for a transfer.'

'But most of those buses are still in the factory,' said Edward. 'It's going to take a while till they come off the production line.'

'Maybe he got the sack,' suggested Jeff.

'You don't get the sack from this job,' said Davy.

'What about Thompson?' I said. 'He got the sack.'

'Oh yes!' retorted Davy. 'You're always mentioning this Thompson who no one else can remember. Go on then! Tell us why he got the sack.'

'He lost patience with his people,' I replied. 'They were complaining he was late when he was actually early, so he drove his bus straight into the vehicle wash and switched the water on.'

'Full of people?'

'Yes,' I said. 'All the windows were open.'

'Good grief,' said Edward. 'No wonder they sacked him.'

'Dismissed on the spot,' I said. 'Hence the expression "An early bath for Thompson".'

'I've never heard that expression,' said Davy.

'You will,' I said. 'You will.'

The bunching of buses posed a question for the authorities that simply would not go away. It remained the Board of Transport's worst headache. The problem was endemic to the extent that there were several collective nouns for buses. These varied according to circumstances. Edward explained them to Jeff and me one day during the mid-morning lull.

'It all depends on the perspective of the observer,' he began. 'For example, whereas drivers might take part in a "convoy of buses", the officials would refer to it as a "liberty of buses". The passengers, meanwhile, view it differently again. For buses nobody wants the correct term is a "procession of buses". When all the buses fly past without stopping it's a "skein of buses"; and then, of course, there's the most prevalent form of all, namely, a "dearth of buses", which is self-explanatory.'

'What about a "fleet of buses"?' proposed Jeff.

'That's for commercial usage only,' Edward replied. 'You can also have a "collection of buses" belonging to private enthusiasts.'

'Doesn't the weather also have some bearing on the matter?' I asked.

'You're quite right,' said Edward. 'In wintry conditions it's a "sludge of buses". On sunny days, by contrast, you might see a "mirage of buses" fading into the distance.'

At that moment the canteen doors swung open and Davy burst in looking very agitated.

'I've had it up to here with Mick Wilson,' he said, indicating his chin. 'I don't know how much more I can take.'

Quickly he ordered breakfast at the counter before coming over to recount his troubles.

'Seven o'clock this morning,' he began, 'I was down in the shed minding my own business, getting my bus ready. I had my seat exactly how I like it; all my mirrors lined up properly; checked the water; everything. I was just settling in when all of a sudden Mick Wilson appeared. He took one look at me and came marching over. "Right," he said, all imperious like. "I need this bus straightaway: out you get!" "Wait a minute," I said, "I've just spent ten minutes getting it ready." "Doesn't matter," said Mick. "You'll have to see the engineers for another one." Then he just commandeered my bus and drove off without so much as a "bye" or "leave".'

Edward gave Davy a penetrating look. For a moment I thought he was about to correct his diction, but then for some reason he changed his mind.

'That must have made you late,' he said.

'Course it made me late,' Davy replied. 'You know how I hate being late.'

We all sympathised: we all hated being late.

'It seems our predictions about Mick have turned out to be true,' said Edward. 'He's only been an inspector for a few weeks and already it's gone to his head.'

'I wonder why he wanted the bus so urgently?' said Jeff.

'Oh,' I said. 'I think I heard Greeves mention there were too many buses up the cross and not enough down the outpost. Mick must have overreacted to the situation.'

'So what's the future going to hold if he carries on like that?' said Davy. 'It'll be untenable.'

'You needn't worry about the future,' said Edward. 'Roadside officials are being phased out.'

'How come?'

'There's going to be a satellite launched in the next few months. Henceforth, the progress of buses will be monitored from outer space.'

'You're joking,' said Davy. 'The Board of Transport couldn't launch a frying pan into space, let alone a satellite.'

'It's not the Board launching it,' Edward explained. 'It's an international project, connecting every bus service in every country. The Board of Transport is just one of a number of subscribers.'

'Funny, isn't it?' said Jeff. 'I can't imagine them having buses in other countries. Only this one.'

'Well, I can assure you there are buses on all five continents,' said Edward. 'I should know. I've studied them.'

'When?'

'During my holidays.'

'You probably know more about buses than the officials,' I remarked.

'Probably,' said Edward. 'Though I do try to share my findings.'

'Do they have double-deckers in these other countries?' Davy enquired.

'In one or two places, yes,' answered Edward. 'Their bus of preference, however, is the single-decker.'

'Didn't they invent the articulated bus?'

'Yes they did: they're pioneers in innovation; but to tell the truth, the general picture is entirely different.'

'How do you mean?'

'There's no "presumption of lateness" in other countries,' said Edward. 'Over here the people presume we're late when, in fact, we're much more likely to be early. Our foreign counterparts, on the other hand, are always presumed to be on time.'

'Blimey!' exclaimed Davy.

'I heard recently they have a 97 per cent efficiency rating, compared to 42 per cent in this country.'

'Well, how are we going to compete with them?' I asked.

'Fortunately, we don't have to compete with anybody,' Edward replied. 'They run their buses over there and we run ours over here. There's no direct competition.'

'That's alright then.'

'Buses will never change in this country,' he continued. 'They'll never get better and they'll never get worse: they'll simply remain the same forever. Oh, certain attempts have been made in the past to bring about improvements. The maintenance of headway was one such crusade, and there have been many others. Yet whatever measures are put in place, in this country they ultimately fail. True, you can calculate the movements of buses just as you can the motions of the stars and planets. What you cannot calculate, however, is the behaviour of people. Shall I go on?'

'You might as well,' I said. 'Now you've started.'

'I'm talking about people who hail buses they don't want,' said Edward. 'People who haven't got the correct fare. People who get on buses just because they happen to be loitering near a bus stop. People who clamour to get on buses that are already full. People who expect buses to wait for them. People who attempt to "hold" the bus by blocking the doorway. People who ring the bell for no good reason. People who try to change buses mid-stream. Argumentative people. People who cross the road when they shouldn't. Cyclists. Cabbies. People who park their vans in bus lanes. People who repair water mains inadequately. People whose occupation is emptying dustbins. The people in charge of traffic lights. And finally, of course, people who drive buses for a living.'

I glanced at my watch, stood up and walked away from the table. It was time for me to go. Edward was still delivering his exposition as I descended the stairs and went in search of my next bus.

He was quite correct. It was people of one kind or another who ultimately disrupted the bus service. Sometimes I even wondered whether they wanted buses in the first place: I was once driving up the rise towards the common with about forty people on board when suddenly my bus ran out of diesel and stopped. Without exception, the entire load of passengers got out of the bus and walked away, all in different directions. As I watched them disperse I was unable to answer the question: what are we here for?

Nevertheless, Edward's extensive theories dealt only with one side of the coin. The other side concerned the matters raised by Breslin. He, too, was correct in his own way. The entire bus network was an enormous apparatus designed to run like clockwork. Despite everyone's best efforts, occasionally the mechanism became clogged up and needed a prod. This, he argued, was the purpose of the officials. It was reassuring to know that he thought of himself not as a tyrant but as a lubricating agent. However, I could foresee little change in that department either.

My bus arrived at the takeover point precisely on time. Now all I had to do was drive it down to the outpost, up to the cross, then back here, and my duties for the day would be complete. With this in mind I sallied forth, paying little regard to the exact details of the schedule. As long as I didn't get too close to the bus in front, I reasoned, then headway would be maintained (more or less).

I was mildly surprised, therefore, when I reached the southern outpost and a figure appeared on the pavement, urgently flagging me down.

It was Jason. He was wearing the smart black uniform of a fully-fledged inspector of buses.

'You're early,' he said. 'Why's that?'

a note on the author

Magnus Mills is the author of two collections of stories and
five novels, including *The Restraint of Beasts*, which won the
McKitterick Prize and was shortlisted for both the Booker
Prize and the Whitbread First Novel Award in 1999. His
other novels are *The Scheme for Full Employment*, *All Quiet
on the Orient Express*, *Three to See the King* and *Explorers of the
New Century*. His books have been translated into twenty
languages. He lives in London.

a note on the type

The text of this book is set in Bembo. This type was first used in 1495 by the Venetian printer Aldus Manutius for Cardinal Bembo's *De Aetna*, and was cut for Manutius by Francesco Griffo. It was one of the types used by Claude Garamond (1480–1561) as a model for his Romain de L'Université, and so it was the forerunner of what became standard European type for the following two centuries. Its modern form follows the original types and was designed for Monotype in 1929.